DASH

ALSO BY KIRBY LARSON

Novels

Audacity Jones to the Rescue

Duke

Liberty

The Friendship Doll

Hattie Big Sky

Hattie Ever After

Dear America: *The Fences Between Us*

Picture Books
with Mary Nethery

Nubs: The True Story of a Mutt, a Marine & a Miracle

*Two Bobbies: A True Story of Hurricane Katrina,
Friendship, and Survival*

KIRBY LARSON

SCHOLASTIC INC.

In honor of the real Mitsi, Mitsue Shiraishi, and the 120,000 heroes like her sent to US incarceration camps during World War II

Nidoto Nai Yoni ~ Let It Not Happen Again

This book was originally published in hardcover by Scholastic Press in 2014.

All rights reserved. Published by Scholastic Inc., *Publishers since 1920*. SCHOLASTIC and associated logos are trademarks and/or registered trademarks of Scholastic Inc.

The publisher does not have any control over and does not assume any responsibility for author or third-party websites or their content.

This book is a work of fiction. Names, characters, places, and incidents are either the product of the author's imagination or are used fictitiously, and any resemblance to actual persons, living or dead, business establishments, events, or locales is entirely coincidental.

ISBN 978-0-545-41636-8

10 9 8 7 6 5 4   16 17 18 19 20

Printed in the U.S.A.   40
First printing 2016

Book design by Whitney Lyle

TABLE OF CONTENTS

CHAPTER ONE

Slanty Eyes

Mitsi Kashino packed her sketch pad, her binder, and her worry in her book bag. Dash sniffed the straps before flattening himself on top of it, muzzle resting on his front paws. He watched Mitsi with worried brown eyes. She ruffled the scruffy almond-colored fur on his head.

"I wish I could tuck you inside." Dash had no idea that Christmas vacation was over, that it was time for Mitsi to go back to school. She lifted a blue headband from her dresser, and paused in front of the mirror before slipping it over her straight black hair. Things might be better, now that more time had passed. Maybe there'd be an end to the mean notes in her desk and funny looks in the hall. Maybe school could be back to normal, even if nothing else was.

Mitsi wrestled her book bag out from under Dash, whose tail wagged hopefully. She rubbed those floppy ears that looked like they'd been dipped in Obaachan's tea. He whimpered so she picked him up, rubbing her cheek against his fur, soft as a baby blanket. "It'll be fine, won't it?"

Dash licked her chin. "Thanks, buddy." She squeezed him again, then put him on the floor. "You stay, now." She motioned with her hand. "I'll see you later."

Ted left for school before her, so Mitsi slipped out the front door by herself, blocking her ears to Dash's whimpers. With book bag and umbrella in hand, she raced down the front steps. She didn't want to be late meeting Mags and Judy. They always went away for the holidays — Mags to her grandma's, and Judy to her aunt and uncle's — so it had been two whole weeks since they'd seen one another. Usually, they were inseparable, like Betsy, Tacy, and Tib in those books. Mitsi didn't even know what her friends had gotten for Christmas! She couldn't wait to tell them what she'd found under her tree: a brand-new sketch pad and a box of chalk pastels. The kind real artists use. Mitsi had spent hours on the pictures tucked in her sketch pad. There were several of Dash — one of him curled up on her bed.

One of him watching Mom cook, waiting for some morsel of food to drop. And one of him dancing in a circle, begging for a treat. She'd also drawn a couple of dragons to match the stories Mags was always writing. Mags would get a kick out of those.

Mitsi ran the last half block to the meet-up bench on Jackson Street. She plunked down on the slatted seat, scrunching her shoulders up toward her ears against the weather. Despite the chill, it warmed her to think how much Judy and Mags would like her drawings. She swung her legs back and forth to get the blood flowing. They should be here any minute now. Pop had said there might be a little snow this week. Mitsi buttoned the top button on her coat.

"*Ohayo!*" Mrs. Kusakabe called from across the street.

Mitsi called hello back to her elderly neighbor, who stopped to lean on her cane.

"Poor Dash will be lonely with you gone all day."

"He'll be okay." Mitsi tried not to think about those sad brown eyes.

"Study hard, now." With a wave, Mrs. Kusakabe hobbled inside Cheeky's café for her breakfast. Mitsi swung her legs faster. If Judy and Mags didn't hurry up, they'd all be tardy. She blew into her cupped hands. She'd been in such a rush, she'd forgotten to grab her mittens.

Too cold to sit any longer, Mitsi marched around the bench — one, two, three laps — stomping hard to warm up her feet. Her nose began to run. Where were they?

Eight, nine, ten laps. She paced to the curb and leaned out into the street, looking left and right. She blew on her hands again, trying not to worry. There'd been a bad cold going around. Maybe Mags and Judy had caught it. She checked the time on the big clock outside Higo 10¢ Store. If she didn't scoot now, she'd be tardy for sure. After one last glance in each direction, Mitsi bolted toward school, arriving seconds before the Pledge of Allegiance. As she stood with her classmates, she caught sight of Mags's red curls and Judy's blonde pageboy. They weren't absent after all. But why hadn't they been at the bench? She'd have to wait until first recess to find out.

Miss Wyatt picked up a basket from her desk. "I have a little New Year's gift for each of you. Patty, you're the room monitor this week. Would you please pass these out?"

Mitsi leaned forward, nearly out of her seat, trying to see what was in the basket.

Roy Biddle reached in first. "A pencil." He wiggled it between his fingers.

"A fresh pencil for a fresh start in the new year." Miss Wyatt beamed.

"Oh." Roy put it in the pencil tray on his desk. His "thanks" didn't sound all that thankful.

Patty handed one to Judy and then to Hudson Young. She worked her way down Mitsi's row. When Patty got to Eddie Munson's desk, right in front of her, Mitsi held out her hand, ready for her pencil. But Patty brushed by.

"Hey, you forgot me," Mitsi said.

Patty turned back. "Oh. Sor-ry." She held out a pencil. It dropped before Mitsi could take it. "Oops." Patty continued passing out pencils.

"She did that on purpose," Grace Arai whispered.

Mitsi shrugged.

"Did everyone get one?" asked Miss Wyatt. Patty showed her the empty basket. "Good. Let's pull out our arithmetic books." Miss Wyatt held out a piece of chalk. "Who would like to solve problem number one?" Several hands shot up.

Spelling followed arithmetic: ten sentences using this week's spelling list. As Mitsi was writing a sentence for word number eight, "behavior" — "The behavior of some people is not very nice" — the recess bell finally rang. She grabbed her sketch pad and hopped up.

"Oh, Mitsi," Miss Wyatt called. "Would you wait a moment, please?" Mitsi glanced over her shoulder. Judy and Mags rushed to the cloakroom with the rest of the class to grab coats and jackets.

She edged to the doorway, ready to dash herself as soon as her teacher was done speaking with her.

"Come here, dear." Miss Wyatt waved her closer.

Mitsi held back a sigh of exasperation. She'd already waited so long to show Judy and Mags her drawings. But she stepped forward.

"I am going to be speaking to all the . . ." Miss Wyatt cleared her throat. "But I wanted to speak to you first." She picked up a pencil and then set it down again. "Things must be very confusing for you right now."

How did Miss Wyatt know about Judy and Mags? Mitsi nodded.

"We're all still part of the same school family, all part of the same community," Miss Wyatt continued. "No matter what happens in the world, nothing can change that."

Mitsi's stomach knotted. This was about that terrible day.

"Do you understand what I'm saying?" Miss Wyatt's hazel eyes brimmed with kindness.

Mitsi nodded again. Anything to escape.

"That's fine, then." Miss Wyatt smiled. "Go on out and play."

Cheeks burning, Mitsi ran outside, straight to the old maple tree where she and Judy and Mags always played jacks.

"Is it too late to get in the game?" Mitsi asked.

"Jacks is for babies." Patty had pushed her way to the spot between Judy and Mags. Sitting where Mitsi always sat. Patty opened a small blue autograph book. They were the newest fad with the sixth-grade girls. None of the fifth graders had one yet. Until now.

"I'm even going to ask Miss Wyatt to sign it." Patty handed Judy a fountain pen.

"I've never written in one of these before." Judy chewed on her lip. "I don't know what to say."

"I know one. It's what my brother writes when the junior high girls ask him to sign their books." Mags jumped up to recite: "The mother put the kid to bed because it wouldn't mind. But when he left I saw he had a little bear behind." She cracked up.

"Mags!" Judy looked horrified.

Mitsi thought it was pretty funny, too. She could see Mags's brother writing that. He was a real card. She thought about what she would sign. Maybe she'd flip to one of the blue pages and write, "I hope you are never the color of this page." She'd heard that in a movie.

Judy leaned over the autograph book, turned to a pink page, and moved the pen across the paper.

"What's it say?" Mags tried to read upside down.

"Make new friends, but keep the old," Judy said. "One is silver and the other gold."

"Oh, that's so sweet." Patty took the book from Judy and held it out to Mags. "Your turn."

"Something nice." Judy leaned over Mags's shoulder.

The pen jogged across the page in Mags's loopy style. "There." Mags put the cap back on the pen.

"Let me see." Patty grabbed the book and read aloud. "'When twilight draws her curtains, and pins them with a star, remember me, your friend dear Patty, though you may wander far.'" She nodded, then slapped the book shut. "I'm going to ask Cindy to sign it next."

Mitsi shifted her sketch pad to her other arm. "But I didn't get a turn."

Patty tossed her pageboy curls. "Come on, you two."

Mitsi turned to her friends.

Mags's expression reminded Mitsi of the times when Dash got caught chewing on Pop's socks. Judy didn't meet Mitsi's gaze at all. And neither of them said a word. Not to Patty. Not to *her*.

"Cindy! Cindy!" Patty flounced off. Judy grabbed Mags's arm and they followed.

Mitsi stood there shivering and alone, wishing she *had* packed Dash in her book bag. What happened on December 7 hadn't changed the way he felt about Mitsi. Not one whit. Why couldn't it be the same for people?

At lunchtime, the cafeteria lady set a plate of meat loaf, mashed potatoes, and gravy on Mitsi's tray. "Pudding or Jell-O?" she asked. Mitsi pointed to a cup of tapioca with a maraschino cherry plopped on top. She paid for lunch, then hesitated. She'd never had to think about where to sit before. She and Mags and Judy had a favorite joke: No matter what was on the menu, the three of them always had a Mitsi sandwich for lunch, with Mitsi right between her two best friends.

Mags caught Mitsi's eye and smiled her regular gap-toothed Mags smile, dimpled and wide. Relieved, Mitsi headed toward their table.

For the second time that day, Patty Tibbets beat her out, settling herself on a stool.

"Uh, that's where Mitsi sits," Mags said.

"I was here first." Patty popped the lid off her milk bottle.

Mags leaned forward, glancing down the table at Judy.

Judy blinked hard. But she didn't tell Patty to move.

Patty pointed across the room to the table where Kenji Hayashi, Grace Arai, and some of the other kids from Mitsi's neighborhood were sitting. "You belong over there."

Mitsi stared at her two best friends. "But this is our table."

Judy squirted ketchup on her meat loaf. Mags concentrated on unwrapping her straw.

Patty put a pointer finger at the outer corner of each of her blue eyes. She pushed her eyelids up into slants and mouthed a word that turned Mitsi's stomach. The word slapped Mitsi back to that horrible Sunday.

Her whole family had been in the living room, listening to the New York Philharmonic on the radio after church. Mitsi and Pop were reading the funnies aloud to each other. It was Mitsi's turn to read *Dick Tracy*, but an announcer cut into the music.

"Hush a minute." Pop signaled Ted to turn up the volume.

"*The Japanese have attacked Pearl Harbor,*" the announcer said.

"Oh no!" Mom pressed her apron hem to her mouth. Pop grabbed the back of his neck with his hands. Ted shook his head *no-no-no*. Obaachan rocked. Even Dash froze, ears perked, listening.

Crazy words ricocheted around the living room, words about Japanese planes flying out of nowhere, dropping bombs, destroying planes, ships. The *Utah*, the *Oklahoma*, the *Arizona*. Lost.

"All those soldiers. All those boys," Mom had sobbed. The next morning, the FBI swept through *Nihonmachi*, Japantown, arresting dozens of businessmen, including their neighbor Mr. Iseri.

That night, someone threw a rock through the plate-glass windows at the Arais' grocery store. Right away the newspapers stopped using the word "Japanese" and started using the word Patty said. "Jap." When the neighbors burned their Japanese books, Mom decided they should, too. Even Great-grandfather's scroll paintings. The rice paper crackled in the burn barrel, as snakes of black smoke slithered into the gray December sky. Obaachan kept repeating, "*Shikata ga nai*. It cannot be helped." But Mom cried as she tossed book after book into the flames.

Now, in the lunchroom, Mitsi fought back tears, too.

She wanted to say, "I was born here in Seattle. At Swedish Hospital, just like you, Mags." She wanted to say, "I have brown eyes, just like you, Judy." She wanted to say, "I have never even been to Japan." But these were things she shouldn't have to say. Not to friends.

Her lunch tray felt as heavy as her heart. Somehow, she made it across the room and slid onto the bench next to Grace. Somehow, she made it through lunch. And, somehow, she managed to do it without tears.

• • •

Right before the last bell, Miss Wyatt handed back their Expert Reports. Mitsi had titled hers "Dogs: Everyone's Best Friend." An A+ stood at attention at the top of her report, in Miss Wyatt's special green ink. Mitsi glanced across the aisle. Patty's paper earned a fat green C. Good.

"What are you doing after school?" Mitsi put her A+ report in her book bag.

Mags took a long time buckling her galoshes. "Nothing," she said.

Judy scooted past, so close that one of her braids

brushed Mitsi's shoulder. She grabbed it and gave it a playful tug.

Judy stared at Mitsi like she was the swamp monster from that scary movie they'd seen. Patty grabbed Judy's arm. "Come on." And Judy went. As if every day since first grade, she and Mags and Mitsi hadn't walked home from school together, to the corner of 6th and Jackson, where they headed north and Mitsi headed south.

Mitsi reached for the red umbrella Ted had given her for Christmas. Red to match Dash's collar. She tucked it under her arm, trying to tune out Patty's loud voice.

"Do you want to go to the show this weekend?" she was asking.

Mitsi couldn't hear the answer, but why wouldn't Mags and Judy say yes? Mr. Tibbets owned the Atlas Theatre, and Patty got all the free Milk Duds she wanted.

Outside, Mitsi paused to pop open her umbrella, to shield herself from the pelting rain. Judy and Mags had never even liked Patty! And now they were acting all cozy, as if the three of *them* were Betsy, Tacy, and Tib. And Mags hated Milk Duds.

Mitsi skirted around a puddle. It used to be that her friends thought Japanese things — like Obaachan's kimonos and *Hina Matsuri* — were nifty. Last year, Judy and Mags had come over before the party to set out the *hina* dolls and help make the rice balls. Now, they were taking sides with Patty Tibbets. There wasn't a red umbrella big enough to shield Mitsi from that kind of rain.

A few blocks from home, she passed some junior high boys hanging out in front of the Higo 10¢ Store, pretending to smoke candy cigarettes. "Hey!" one of them called out to her.

Mitsi didn't answer. She kept walking.

The boys followed.

She walked faster.

They walked faster.

Mitsi ran. They ran.

Right in front of the Nelsons' old house, Mitsi tripped and fell. Her book bag went flying. A boy in a plaid jacket snatched it up and yanked out Mitsi's report. "Aww. Iddin dat sweet? A paper about doggies." He ripped it into shreds, tossing them into the air. "Look, it's snowing!"

A scrap with Miss Wyatt's green ink words —

Another fine job, Mitsi — landed on Mitsi's coat. The boy dumped the book bag out on the soggy ground.

A second boy kicked her books into a puddle. All of them. Even her new sketch pad.

Knees stinging, Mitsi pushed herself up off the sidewalk. Blood oozed around the edges of the ragged holes in her stockings. Tears boiled at the back of her eyes.

"Serves you right." The boy in the plaid jacket glared. He and his buddies formed a ring around her. "Remember Pearl Harbor, remember Pearl Harbor," they chanted.

Mitsi turned around on wobbly legs. She tried to duck under their linked arms, but the boys bounced her back to the center of the circle like a beach ball. The sour taste of fear hit the back of her throat. There were too many of them. How would she get out?

"OWWWWW!" The boy in the plaid jacket jumped back, holding his head. "What the —?"

Beyond the boys, an old lady wearing big black rubber boots waved a broom. "Shame on you."

"We were just kidding around," said one of the boys.

"What are you? A Jap lover?" asked another.

The lady lifted the broom handle to her shoulder, like a baseball player, ready to swing again. For an old lady, she looked strong.

The circle fell apart.

She stamped a rubber-booted foot. "Now, get on home. Before I call your mothers."

The boy who'd gotten the clop stood there a minute, rubbing his head. "Aww, let's get out of here, guys." He ambled down the street, with the others hot on his heels.

The old lady leaned her broom against the fence. "Hooligans." She wiped off the sketch pad with a flowered apron that was tied over her coat. "Let it dry, then put it under something heavy. That will iron out most of the wrinkles." She stepped closer, holding it out to Mitsi. "Oh, my. Look at your knee."

Mitsi didn't want to look. She wanted to get home. "It's okay." She took the pad.

The lady gathered up the rest of the books and papers. Mitsi brushed off her book bag and held it open. The lady dropped everything inside, then bent over to pick up a few soggy scraps of Mitsi's report.

"Dogs." She smiled, looking at the title. "I love them but don't have one."

"I do." Mitsi latched the straps on her book bag. "Dash."

"Good name for a dog." The lady nodded. "Speaking of names, mine is Mrs. Bowker."

Mitsi told Mrs. Bowker her name, too.

"Well, isn't that pretty? Suits you to a T." Mrs. Bowker patted Mitsi's arm. "You'd best get on home before your mother worries." She picked up her broom again. "I'll watch while you walk the rest of the way."

Mitsi clutched her book bag. "Thank you."

Mrs. Bowker was right. The papers would dry. And putting them under something heavy would smooth out the wrinkles. Mitsi had done that before.

But wrinkles like Judy and Mags and looking like the enemy? She had no idea how to iron those out.

CHAPTER TWO

Friends and Foes

Ted had his paper route, Pop had work, and Mom was in bed with a terrible cold. "I wouldn't ask you." Mom nibbled at the *umeboshi*, pickled sour plum, that Obaachan fed them whenever they got sick. "But it's the last day to register."

So there Mitsi was, sitting on a city bus next to her grandmother. She rested against the window, head jiggling along with the bus's vibrations. As it turned left at Jackson, leaving Nihonmachi to bump north on 2nd Avenue, Mitsi saw more and more white faces. A drugstore near the Smith Tower wore a big sign in its front window: WE DON'T SERVE JAPS. She turned away and leaned into Obaachan's wool coat. Breathed deeply of her grandmother's warm rosewater scent. After a few more blocks, at Union Street, Mitsi pulled the cord, and the driver stopped. Obaachan held her cane in one hand and her pocketbook in the other. Mitsi helped her off the bus and into the post office, where they followed the signs down to the Registration Room in the basement.

Right after Christmas, they'd had to turn in their cameras and radios. Mitsi had been so sad to see the old Gloritone go. No more *Blondie* or *Gasoline Alley* or *Lone Ranger* radio shows after school. Now there was this new rule about Alien Registration. Anybody born in Germany, Italy, or Japan had to get a card that said they weren't American. Mitsi didn't know what happened if you didn't get the card. Maybe the FBI would come take you away. Like Mr. Iseri. The morning after Pearl Harbor, three men in dark suits and fedoras had escorted him down his front steps and into a big sedan parked in front of Mitsi's house.

Mom said it was all a big mistake. Mr. Iseri had traveled to Japan the year before, hoping to sell Washington apples. But the FBI thought he was mixed up in being a spy or something and arrested him. He and a bunch of other men from Nihonmachi had been sent to a place called Fort Missoula. So far, Mrs. Iseri had heard from him only once, a letter that looked like a piece of Swiss cheese because of all the places where the censors had razored out what he'd written.

After Mr. Iseri was taken away, every time Pop went to a church meeting at night, Mitsi had nightmares, imagining what might happen if someone made a mistake about *him*. What if the FBI thought the deacons of the Baptist church were helping the emperor? What if Pop got arrested like Mr. Iseri and the others? Got sent away? Thank goodness he had never, ever been to Japan.

But Obaachan was born there. And lived there until she was sixteen, when Grandfather saw a photograph of her and decided they should get married. They didn't even know each other! He sent for her and she'd been in Seattle ever since. Mitsi wasn't sure how many years it had been, but it was a long, long time. Obaachan would never do anything to help Japan. She was a Rainiers fan, wasn't she? Loving baseball was as all-American as you could get.

The Registration Room reminded Mitsi of Ted's old ant farm, but crawling with humans instead of ants. And humid and stuffy from all the people in their damp wool coats. Noisy, too. All around her whirled snippets of German, Italian, and Japanese. Lots and lots of Japanese. She led Obaachan to the end of the nearest line and they waited. And waited. And waited. Finally, it was their turn.

The man behind the desk asked for Obaachan's photographs. "You have three, right?" He didn't even look up.

Mitsi didn't know the Japanese word for photographs. She didn't know much Japanese at all. She held her hands up around her face, like a frame.

Obaachan's face wrinkled in confusion.

"Look," said the man, "I gotta lot of people behind you. Snap it up."

Mitsi pointed to the pocketbook. "May I open it?"

Obaachan nodded. Mitsi looked inside and found an envelope with three photographs. With a grunt, the man took them. Then he machine-gunned questions at Obaachan — When were you born? Where? How tall are you? What do you weigh? Mitsi translated and he wrote down the answers on a paper in front of him: March 9, 1859. Okayama, Japan. Five feet. Eighty-eight pounds. Then he grunted again. Without even asking, he reached over and grabbed Obaachan's right hand. He pressed her index finger onto a big black ink pad, then onto a small square on a green card. Obaachan stared straight ahead, as if this was happening to someone else. Her lips were a straight line, like the obi, the sash, on her kimono.

Mitsi swallowed hard, trying to wash away the bad taste in her mouth. In the movies, the only people who got fingerprinted were criminals. Not grandmothers.

"Next." The man motioned for Mitsi and Obaachan to move out of the way.

Obaachan opened her pocketbook again and took out a handkerchief. She wiped at the ink on her finger, but the black smudge lingered.

"It will wash off," Mitsi assured her, even though she didn't know if that was true. She pushed open the door to step outside. The cool air was a relief. Mitsi breathed deep.

"Ice cream?" Obaachan pointed her cane toward Woolworth's, across the street.

Mitsi flashed back on that sign she'd seen from the bus. But there was no such sign in the Woolworth's window. "Okay." They waited for traffic to pass, then crossed. Mitsi reached to open the door for Obaachan, but it opened on its own. Someone was coming out.

Mitsi froze. It was Patty Tibbets, with her mother.

"Well, hello, Mitsi." Mrs. Tibbets smiled. Too bad none of her niceness ever rubbed off on Patty. "On an outing with your grandmother? How lovely!"

Mitsi nodded. Obaachan returned Mrs. Tibbets's greeting with a bow. "Lubly," she repeated.

Patty snickered. Quietly. Mrs. Tibbets didn't react.

Mitsi felt her cheeks go hot to hear her grandmother's funny English through Patty's ears. And to see the way she tapped her cane when she walked. And that black mark on her finger.

Mrs. Tibbets said good-bye, and they were gone. But Patty's snicker lingered. Stiffly, Mitsi followed Obaachan to the counter, where they took two empty stools. Obaachan ordered a dish of strawberry ice cream for each of them.

"Good?" Obaachan watched Mitsi take the first taste.

"Good," she lied. Mitsi didn't taste the strawberries. Only shame.

. . .

Dash jumped on the bed and snuggled against Mitsi's back, tucking his neck over hers. Mitsi breathed in his warm coppery scent. He was a soft, furry blanket of love, keeping her warm and safe. Usually, he helped her forget her problems. Reading helped, too. But she'd been staring at the pages of *Caddie Woodlawn* since they'd gotten back from the post office, and all she could see in front of her eyes was a green card with a black fingerprint. And Patty's smirk.

Mitsi shifted to her back. Dash snuffled and readjusted, curling up at her side. Patty. If she were an animal, she'd be a rat. All squinty eyed, and sneaky. "Maybe I should sic you on her." Dash caught a rat once, at Uncle Shig's farm. He'd chased it under the chicken coop, dragged it out, and dispatched it with a couple of hard shakes. Uncle Shig had been so happy to have the rat gone, he'd given Dash a bone as a reward.

"A real rat is one thing. A human rat is another." Mitsi looked into Dash's eyes, trying to imagine what would happen if she turned him loose on

Patty. He licked her chin. "That's probably what you'd do, isn't it? Give her a kiss." She scratched behind his ears. "You're so ferocious."

That's why the whole thing with the rat had been so surprising to Mitsi. Dash would never hurt a soul. Not even someone who deserved it. Like Patty. If Judy and Mags had heard her make fun of Obaachan, they would've dropped her like a hot biscuit. Obaachan had taught Judy how to knit so she could earn her Brownie badge for home arts. And how many times had she folded origami animals to match the stories Mags made up? "I have three grandmas," Mags told people. "Grandma Dot, Grandma Millie, and Obaachan."

Mitsi heard the back door slam, then sounds of Ted banging around in his bedroom on the other side of the wall. He bounded into her room. "Want to see my new magic trick?" He waved a fan of cards at her.

"You forgot to knock."

Ted rapped on Mitsi's forehead. "There."

She shoved his hand away. "Very funny." She picked up her book again.

"Come on. Let me do the trick," he begged. "It's really nifty."

"Where'd you get a new one? I thought you were broke."

"I won the subscription contest." He grinned. "I signed up the most new subscribers in a month. Even got that new lady, Mrs. Bowker." Ted leaned against the desk. "It was kind of funny. She knew we had a dog named Dash." He shrugged. "And we haven't even met her before."

Mitsi traced the pattern in her chenille bedspread, eyes down. She didn't want Ted to know what happened that day. He might tell Mom or Pop. Or, worse, go after those boys himself. She thought as fast as she could. "Well, Mom said she'd met her at the grocery store. Maybe *she* told her." At least the first part of Mitsi's answer was true. "So, what's this big new trick?" She leaned forward, acting really interested.

"Take a gander at these cards." The fan Ted held out contained a black 3, 5, 7, and 10, with a red queen between the 5 and the 7. "Got 'em?"

She nodded.

Ted flipped the fan around and handed her a paper clip. "Clip this on the queen."

"Piece of cake." She slid the paper clip over the middle card.

"Are you sure?" He waggled his eyebrows like Groucho Marx.

How dumb did he think she was? The queen was in the middle. "I'm sure."

Ted waved his hand over the fan and, with a flourish, turned the cards to face her.

She'd paper-clipped the 3, not the queen, even though it was still in the middle.

"Not so easy!" Ted flapped the fan under her nose.

She grabbed the cards from him. "How'd you do that?"

"Magicians never reveal their secrets." He grabbed the cards back. "Let's just say, things aren't always as they seem."

"Yeah, yeah, yeah." Mitsi waved him away. Sometimes, Ted was pretty full of himself. "If you're such a good magician, why don't you make yourself disappear?"

"If I did, you'd have to set the table tonight." He sauntered out of the room.

Mitsi hurled her book after him. "It'd be worth it!"

Dash climbed into her lap. "Brothers!" She stroked Dash's head. "Be thankful you don't have one."

Ted thought he was the cat's meow, tricking her like that. All that "things are not always as they seem" mumbo jumbo. He'd seen too many Houdini movies. "Magic." She fluffed the fur between Dash's ears and pushed him off her lap. If Ted really wanted to do a good trick, he would turn Mags and Judy back into her best friends.

She walked across the room to pick up poor old *Caddie Woodlawn*. Things aren't always as they seem. She took hold of the book, then jerked upright. What if she was misreading what was going on with Mags and Judy, just like she'd misread where the queen was? Maybe they were confused, too, about Pearl Harbor and everything, and were just waiting for her to be the same old Mitsi. So they could be the same old Mags and Judy.

"I am so dense!" She tossed the book on her desk. "If I want things to be back to normal, I need to *act* like they are." Dash pawed at her legs, begging to be picked up. She scooped him up and danced around the room. Valentine's Day was right around the corner. She knew just what to do to win her friends back.

Patty Tibbets would have to find a new place to sit at lunchtime.

CHAPTER THREE

Hearts and Flowers

A new sign hung in the window of Wong's Restaurant: CHINESE. It wasn't the only one Mitsi saw as she walked to school. Maybe half a dozen windows had the same sign taped to the glass. It was all because some people couldn't tell the difference between Chinese and Japanese. And it sure wasn't good to be Japanese right now. Pop said Cheeky's lunch crowd had dropped off to nothing. Cheeky made the best ten-don in Seattle, charging only seventy-five cents for a big bowl of shrimp and rice, but the downtown businessmen weren't coming anymore. Pop said Cheeky might have to close the café.

Mitsi slowed her step as she approached the meet-up bench. She couldn't help it; it was an old habit even though no one had been there since before Christmas break. That would change after today. Mitsi was sure of it.

She shifted her book bag to her other shoulder, careful of the valentine cards inside. Yesterday, she'd cut out thirty red construction-paper hearts, decorating them with bits of lace and paper doilies. There were two more valentines in her bag as well, peek-a-boo cards, with her photo tucked inside a special flap. She and Mags and Judy had been making these cards for one another since first grade, when all three of them wore big smiles with missing baby teeth. Mitsi had a page ready in her scrapbook for this year's photos of her best friends.

At school, Miss Wyatt acted as though it was any old ordinary day, carrying on with spelling and reading and social studies. She even gave a pop quiz on long division! Mitsi thought she might burst if she had to wait one more minute. Finally, finally, Miss Wyatt set the chalk in the blackboard tray. "Shall we distribute our valentines?" she asked. "I'll go first."

Up and down the rows she walked, sliding a card through the decorated shoe box on each student's desk.

When she reached the last seat in the last row, she clapped her hands. "All right, my little Cupids. Your turn!"

Kids popped up like exploding popcorn kernels, dashing around the room.

Roy Biddle hesitated next to Judy's desk. Mitsi noticed he was holding an envelope behind his back. Patty noticed, too.

"Judy and Roy, sittin' in a tree," she sang.

Judy's face turned as red as a licorice rope. Roy's did, too. He shoved the envelope at her, then stomped away. "Mind your own beeswax," he growled at Patty. She just snickered.

Mitsi delivered the last of her cards as the bell rang.

"Happy Valentine's Day, class," Miss Wyatt called out over the commotion. "And don't forget the spelling test on Monday."

In the cloakroom, Cindy Cotrell shook her box noisily. "There must be a million cards in here," she said.

"I bet I have two million," said Patty.

Mitsi's mailbox felt awfully light. She peeked through the slot.

Roy pushed past Patty and she started in on him again. "First comes love, second comes marriage . . ."

"Can it!" Roy whirled around, knocking Judy's

mailbox out of her hands. The lid popped off. Cards flew everywhere.

Mitsi hung back while Judy and Mags picked them up.

"I told you he liked you." Patty scooped a handful of cards off the floor. Judy's face deepened to another shade of red. Mags wrapped her arm around Judy's shoulder, leaning in, whispering something.

"What is this?" Patty held up a small card.

Mitsi's stomach clenched.

"A peek-a-boo card?" Patty wrinkled her nose as if she'd touched a slug. "Who would make such a baby thing?" She threw it down. "Come on, girls. Let's go." Mitsi's card skittered across the floor.

Mitsi hid out in the cloakroom until everyone else was gone, then she picked up the peek-a-boo card and threw it in the trash. What had she been thinking? Outside, the wind whipped her hair around, and moisture dripped off her bangs. She brushed the wet away, then pushed the red umbrella open; it snapped. Turned inside out. Mitsi struggled to set it to rights.

But she felt inside out, too. She hadn't thought the card would be babyish. She was just trying to get things back to normal. Back to Betsy, Tacy, and Tib.

A robin flew past, flapping its wings hard against the gusts. It was alone, too. Mitsi brushed at her wet face again, then ducked her head into the wind.

"Hello, neighbor!" Mrs. Bowker's bright yellow slicker glistened with rain. She stomped a shovel blade into the ground, cutting a new garden bed. "Happy Valentine's Day."

Mitsi stopped. "Happy Valentine's Day."

"I'll bet you're eager to get home to look at all your cards." Mrs. Bowker rested against the shovel handle. "I remember those days." She chuckled. "Though I can't remember the last time I got a valentine."

Mitsi couldn't imagine not even getting *one* card on Valentine's Day.

Mrs. Bowker straightened up, rubbing her lower back. She sighed. "I hope all this work pays off. I keep trying to imagine this" — she nodded at the bare garden — "all abloom, but it's hard to keep the faith in February."

Mitsi leaned against the picket fence. Mrs. Bowker had a point. Seattle winters could be discouraging.

A person needed a flicker of light, of color, of hope. Like a garden. Or a friend.

"What kind of flowers are you going to plant?" she asked.

"Oh, crocus and daffodils and tulips." Mrs. Bowker waved her arm like an orchestra conductor. "And later on, peonies and roses and gladiolus."

Mitsi thought of the beautiful gardens Uncle Shig planted along the borders of his strawberry fields. "It must be hard to wait," she said.

"Oh, very hard." Tears glimmered in Mrs. Bowker's brown eyes. "But that's what life is all about. Doing winter's work in hopes of summer's flowers."

Mitsi shifted her hands on the pickets.

Mrs. Bowker shook herself a bit. "My husband was the gardener in our family. Sometimes, I miss him so much." She scraped mud off her shovel. "Well, I'm going to head in now. See you tomorrow, dear."

At home, Mitsi changed out of her school clothes before presenting Dash with his Milk-Bone valentine. While he crunched away, she opened her mailbox and rummaged through the small pile of cards. She counted: five. Five. And not one was addressed in Mags's big loopy hand, or Judy's tidy upright penmanship. She'd been silly to expect peek-a-boo cards from them; that *was* little-kid stuff. But she thought they would at least give her some kind of card.

Loneliness wrapped around her like a snake. She never, ever dreamed that her friends would desert her like this. How was she going to make it through the rest of the year? The rest of her life?

She peeled open the envelope from Miss Wyatt. The card inside showed an artist standing at an easel. It said, *Picture me happy that you're my valentine.* Mitsi set it on her dresser before opening the rest. There was one that wasn't signed, probably from Hudson Young — he was kind of scatterbrained — along with cards from Kenji and Grace, and Cindy Cotrell. A preacher's kid, Cindy was nice to everyone.

His treat devoured, Dash snuffled at her pockets. "All gone," she said. She pulled him onto her lap. "Well, at least I got five."

Dash snuffled.

"I know." Mitsi scratched behind his ears. "I'm being selfish. Poor Mrs. Bowker didn't get even one card." Dash stretched out his neck and closed his eyes. Mitsi hit his ticklish spot and his leg began to thump. "And she seemed so sad about her husband."

She gave Dash a pat, then set him back on the floor. "I've got an idea." Dash followed her to her desk and curled up at her feet. "Let's plant a garden of our own." Placing paper and her new chalk pastels on the desk in front of her, Mitsi tried to remember the flowers Mrs. Bowker had mentioned. She slid out the purple pastel, dabbing it against the lower edge of the paper, for a splash of early-blooming crocuses. She added a dash of yellow for daffodils, and some orange tulips like the ones Uncle Shig grew. She pressed her lips together, sweeping her hand across the paper, again and again. A zigzag of red. A spiral of pink. Thin, short slashes of green, green grass.

"There!" She held the picture out for Dash to admire. "What do you think?" He sniffed, then sneezed. "Gee, thanks." Mitsi studied the picture for a few minutes. She added a bit more green and then, in the bottom right-hand corner, drew a small red heart. Under that, she signed her name.

"Mom, can I take this to Mrs. Bowker?" Mitsi held up the picture.

"That's beautiful, honey." Mom wrapped a loaf of warm bread in a tea towel. "Here, take this, too." Mitsi rolled her picture into a scroll and tied it with one of her hair ribbons. Dash was snoring away in her bedroom, so she decided to let him sleep. She tucked the scroll inside her coat to keep it dry and ran all the way.

Mitsi handed Mrs. Bowker the picture when she opened the door. "I made something for you. Mom did, too." She presented the loaf of bread.

"This looks like the makings of afternoon tea," said Mrs. Bowker. "Come on in. Make yourself at home." She stepped toward the kitchen. "I'll be right back."

Mitsi hadn't been inside Mrs. Bowker's house before. A typewriter, its roller loaded with a piece of yellowed paper, peeked out from behind a stair-stepped pile of books. Over on the piano, ragged stacks of sheet music teetered on the verge of an avalanche. Mitsi would have been grounded if her room ever looked like this. She carefully moved a pile of seed catalogs to make room to sit on the davenport.

"I thought you might prefer Ovaltine to tea." Nudging a couple of *National Geographic*s out of the way, Mrs. Bowker set a pink chintz china cup on the coffee table in front of Mitsi.

Mitsi scooted to the edge of the davenport. "It's my favorite." Mrs. Bowker produced a green glass plate layered with thick slices of Mom's bread spread with butter and some kind of delicious-looking ruby-red jam.

Mrs. Bowker took the chair across from Mitsi, brushing more magazines to the floor. She picked up the scroll. "Shall I open this now?"

Mitsi squirmed. What if Mrs. Bowker thought the picture was dumb? "Oh, you can wait." She licked a blob of jam off her thumb.

But Mrs. Bowker was already untying the ribbon, unrolling the scroll. "Why, this is lovely. Lovely." Her smile melted her wrinkles away. "I'll go over to Higo tomorrow and get a frame. I know right where I'll hang it."

Mitsi hid her grin behind her cup. "Where?"

Mrs. Bowker pointed to a spot above the fireplace mantel. "There, of course! Where I can see it every evening." She carefully rerolled the picture into a scroll. "Ted is not the only magician at your house," she said. "You work magic, too. With your art."

"Really?" Mitsi turned the chintz cup around in her hands. She'd never thought about her art like that before.

"Absolutely." Mrs. Bowker tapped the scroll against her palm. "I smell spring when I look at this. Imagine spring! In February."

Her words warmed Mitsi all the way home.

CHAPTER FOUR

Bad News on the Telephone Pole

Mitsi figured that if she could conjure up a garden on paper, she could use her art to work magic with her friends. She spent a whole week making autograph books for Mags and Judy. They weren't store-bought like Patty's, but Mitsi thought they were just as nice. And not babyish like those peek-a-boo cards. She'd stitched the pages on Mom's Singer machine, sewing a red cover for Mags, yellow for Judy. She'd been so excited to find a scrap of fabric in Mom's sewing basket that almost matched Judy's blonde curls.

When she got to school, Mitsi slipped the two books out of her bag. She peeked into the classroom. Miss Wyatt was nowhere in sight. All clear.

Behind her, kids shuffled around in the cloakroom. She'd have to hurry! Mags's desk was a pigpen. Mitsi moved aside a math book, rearranging a jumble of old spelling tests to make room. When she picked up the last test, she froze.

A stack of notes. *Those* notes. The classroom floor turned to quicksand. Mitsi grabbed a chair to steady herself.

"Mitsi?" Miss Wyatt stood in the doorway. "Are you all right, dear? You look a little peaked."

Mitsi turned to her own desk, shoving the autograph books deep inside. She hadn't gotten a note or a picture in a while, but she'd thought they'd been from Patty. Patty! Never Mags.

"I might be coming down with something," she said.

Mitsi remembered the worst cartoon. It showed a Japanese man with bugged eyes behind round glasses. His huge teeth were sharpened to fangs, dripping blood. Had Mags really cut that out of the newspaper? Put it in Mitsi's desk? Had she written that note with the big red dot above the words *You're a zero, like the planes*? Or the one that said *I'd like to slap your Jap face*? All of them written left-handed or something, so Mitsi wouldn't recognize the writing. And she hadn't. She hadn't.

She fell into her seat, almost feeling guilty for thinking that the note writer had been Patty. Almost.

Miss Wyatt came over and put her hand on Mitsi's forehead. "You do feel a little warm. Would you like to go to the nurse?" She handed Mitsi a handkerchief.

Mitsi couldn't dirty her teacher's hanky. She wiped her tears away with the heels of her hands. "No. No, thank you."

Her classmates began filing in, taking their seats. Miss Wyatt gave Mitsi another questioning look. "Are you sure?" she whispered.

Mitsi nodded. What if the nurse sent her home? That would be one more thing for Mom and Pop to worry about. And they didn't need one more thing to worry about. Not after the latest news. Pop had worked at the electric company since before Ted was born. His boss, Mr. Adams, had given him a promotion last year. Mr. Adams liked Pop. He took him fishing on his boat. And he always gave them a ham at Christmas. Pop said it wasn't Mr. Adams's fault that he got fired. And it wasn't just Pop; there were about a dozen men. All fired because their names were Kashino, or Ikeda, or Yamada.

After the Pledge of Allegiance, Miss Wyatt pointed to the spelling list on the blackboard. "Take out a piece of paper and begin writing your vocabulary sentences." Mitsi opened her binder and began her ten sentences. Number one: "received." *I received an A on my essay.* Number two: "revenge." *I took revenge on my enemy.* Number three: "reverse." *My dad drove in reverse down the driveway.*

Mitsi stopped. Reread sentence number two. Then she pulled out another piece of paper and slipped it under her vocabulary sheet. Two could play at this game. As she put her pencil to the page, angry words bubbled out, water boiling over a saucepan. She knew Mags so well; it wasn't hard to come up with a note that would jab her in every sore spot. When she was finished, Mitsi looked over what she'd written. It was just as mean and ugly as the notes Mags had written to her. *I took revenge on my enemy.*

When they were dismissed for recess, Mitsi hung back a bit, shuffling oh-so-slowly, until all her classmates were out of the room. With Miss Wyatt's back turned, Mitsi slipped over to Mags's desk.

Wait until Mags got a taste of her own medicine.

Mitsi opened the desk lid with her right hand. The note was in her left. All she had to do was let it drop. Let it drop.

Let it drop.

Mitsi couldn't do it. Pearl Harbor might have changed Mags, but not Mitsi. No matter what anyone thought, she was still the same girl she'd always been. The very same. It gave Mitsi a stomachache to think of being that kind of mean to another person. She couldn't do it. Not even to Patty. Certainly not to Mags.

Mitsi crumpled up the note and shoved it into her skirt pocket. Then she went outside, where Grace trounced her in a game of tetherball.

. . .

For the next few days, Mitsi felt like one of those fish in Uncle Shig's pond every winter. They were only dull orange shadows swimming under the ice. Mitsi went to school each day, stood for the pledge, carried a lunch tray, worked math problems on the chalkboard. But she didn't feel anything. Not when Patty Tibbets made slanty eyes, or when the newspaper blared headlines like ARMY MAY HAVE TO MOVE

BAINBRIDGE JAPS. Or when she found another mean note in her desk. The new Mitsi was too cold, too deep under the water for anything — or anyone — to touch her.

Except for all those memories that swam around with the underwater Mitsi, bumping into her like hungry minnows. Memories of Mags helping her carry Dash the time he got a big thorn in his paw. Or of Mags waiting until a Sunday to see *Pinocchio* at the Atlas Theatre because Mitsi had Japanese school on Saturdays. And what about the time Mags spent her whole allowance on that special art eraser for Mitsi's birthday? How did that Mags turn into the Mags of the mean notes? It was like a complicated story problem in math, one that Mitsi just couldn't puzzle out.

She climbed the front steps, pushing open the front door. "Mom?" She scuffed her saddle shoes across the linoleum floor. Maybe Mom could help her figure it out. She stepped through the doorway, into the kitchen. "Mom?"

Mom waved at Mitsi to be quiet, pointing at the black receiver in her hand. "Uh-huh, uh-huh." She turned her back to Mitsi, nodding as she spoke. It was another one of those whispery telephone conversations she had nearly every day. Mom shooed Mitsi out of the kitchen. Didn't even let her get an after-school snack.

Mitsi changed out of her school clothes, then clipped Dash's leash to his collar for his afternoon walk. At least he was glad to see her. Dash led Mitsi up one street and around the next. He sniffed everything in sight, pausing to bark at Mrs. Kusakabe's cat and to water the street signs on each corner.

Lost in thought, Mitsi jumped when she heard someone call her name.

"I wondered if I'd see you two today." Mrs. Bowker rubbed her shoulder. "I'm getting too old for this." A smudge of mud dotted her cheek. Mitsi rubbed at her own cheek, but Mrs. Bowker didn't pick up on the message. Even though she was smiling, she looked tired. More wrinkled.

Mitsi wound Dash's leash around her hand. "Want some help?"

"You might be sorry you asked!" Mrs. Bowker unlatched the gate and handed Mitsi a spare pair of gardening gloves. "Do you know which ones are weeds?"

"I think so." Mitsi undid Dash's leash so he could run around in the yard. She pointed. "That one, that one, and that one."

Mrs. Bowker rubbed her cheek, making another smudge. "I should have known. Artists make good gardeners."

Mitsi tossed a handful of weeds toward a garden bucket. One dandelion went flying and Dash pounced, picking it up by the roots and shaking it back and forth, as if it were a rat. Dandelion puffs fluttered every which way.

"He looks very proud of himself for killing that weed." Mrs. Bowker laughed.

Mitsi pushed the trowel under a root. "You should see him with Pop's socks!"

Mrs. Bowker yanked up a handful of chickweed. "I can only imagine."

They worked quietly, while Dash — muzzle freckled with dirt, and rhododendron blossoms stuck to his fur — pranced around Mrs. Bowker's yard, pouncing on this weed or that leaf.

Mitsi finished one flower bed, then eased to a stand and shook out her legs. Now she understood why Pop took a long, hot bath when he got home last night. She could imagine what his muscles must feel like after crouching over in Uncle Shig's strawberry fields, hour after hour. But Pop didn't complain.

"You've certainly been a great help." Mrs. Bowker emptied the weed bucket into the trash can. "Go ahead. Scoot. You probably have friends waiting for you."

"Not anymore," Mitsi blurted out. She ducked her head and pulled up another weed.

Mrs. Bowker cocked her head like Dash did sometimes. "A sweet girl like you?"

Mitsi shook her head, biting her bottom lip. Mrs. Bowker wouldn't understand. Her skin was the right color. Her name wasn't Japanese. She never got mean notes.

"Did you know I moved here from Montana?" Mrs. Bowker asked.

"No." Mitsi had never thought about Mrs. Bowker being from somewhere else. Only that she lived here now.

"We — my husband and I — had an automobile dealership there." She smiled, more wrinkles melting away. "My husband was a Dodge man, through and through. I was partial to Nashes myself." Her eyes were looking at something over Mitsi's head, far away. Several seconds passed before she spoke again. "In a small town like ours, you know everyone. Everyone." She tightened her grip on the weed bucket handle. "That's why it never should have happened." Her voice got low and shaky.

"What?" Mitsi rocked back on her heels.

"It's easy to blame the war. All the talk, getting people riled up. But that is no excuse. No excuse at all. God gave us brains to think for ourselves." She tapped the bucket against her leg.

The conversation was a knot that Mitsi was having a hard time untangling. But it seemed best not to interrupt. To let Mrs. Bowker tell her story.

"The Schmidts were good customers. Good friends! How many times did I enjoy a little coffee klatch with Mrs. Schmidt?" Mrs. Bowker shook her head. "But the Great War came. With Germany. And suddenly, the Schmidts and everyone like them were our enemy. We weren't part of it, my husband and I, but they were driven out of town." A tear trickled down Mrs. Bowker's cheek. She didn't seem to notice. "How many years has it been? Twenty-five? And I am still ashamed. I never once defended them. Never once stood by them." She drew in a ragged breath. "It was a bitter lesson to learn about myself."

Mitsi looked at her neighbor. "You're nice," she said. "You helped me with those boys that day."

Mrs. Bowker dropped the empty weed bucket. "Even the kindest of us is capable of cruelty. And I was cruel in not speaking up back then." She peeled off her work gloves. "Let's call it quits for the day, shall we?" Her voice was light and cheery, but her face was painted with sadness. "See you tomorrow?"

Mitsi nodded. "See you tomorrow." She clipped Dash's leash back on and headed for home, turning Mrs. Bowker's story over and over in her mind. It still made her sad after all these years, not helping her friends. Would Judy and Mags be sad, someday, about not standing up for Mitsi? Deep down, they were nice people, too, just like Mrs. Bowker.

Dash tugged on his leash, tugging Mitsi out of her thoughts.

"Hey, sis!" Ted loped down the street toward them. Dash jumped up on him as soon as he got within leash range.

"Where are you going?"

"Collecting." Ted held up his subscription book.

"Can I come?" Anything would be better than sitting at home with her thoughts, trying to tune out Mom's whispered conversations. Mitsi didn't think she could pretend to read one more page of *Caddie Woodlawn*.

Ted grumbled, but he let them tag along. They headed over to Spruce Street, walking up eight blocks and then back down. One of Ted's customers grumbled, saying something about "your kind," as he paid his bill. The man at the very next house gave Ted a twenty-five-cent tip. "You're the best paperboy I've ever had," he told Ted. "I've never had to fish one paper off the roof!"

Ted pocketed the tip.

"How much longer?" Mitsi's feet were itchy-hot inside her Keds.

"All finished." Ted counted up his money. But instead of turning on 12th, toward home, he turned right, onto Fir.

"Where are you going?" Mitsi asked.

Ted flipped the quarter in his hand. "Someplace where I can magically turn *this* into two sodas!"

"Logan's!" Mitsi practically flew down the street to Logan's Drugstore and Soda Fountain.

"Don't tell Mom." A bell jingled as Ted opened the door. "I'll catch heck for wrecking your appetite."

Mitsi held up three fingers and drew a cross over her heart. "Scout's honor!"

She tied Dash to a bench where she could keep an eye on him from inside. The soda jerk set a tall glass in front of each of them. Ted had ordered a Green River. Chocolate soda for Mitsi. She plunged the tip of the long-handled spoon deep into the glass, bringing up a bite of the vanilla ice cream. She always did that. After that first perfect bite, she carefully stirred together the soda water and chocolate syrup and ice cream. But she got only a few sips before Dash started carrying on outside. It was his "here's the mailman" bark.

"That your dog?" asked the soda jerk.

"Go quiet him down." Ted nudged Mitsi off her stool.

She took another quick sip, then slipped outside. "Hey, Dash. What's the matter?" Even though she scratched him in all his favorite places, he wouldn't stop barking. Finally, she saw what he was barking at.

It wasn't a mailman but a man in another kind of uniform. Actually, there were two men, a block or so away. Soldiers. They moved from telephone pole to telephone pole, hammering up posters. Dash growled as the men drew near.

One of the soldiers reached out to pet him. "What's your name, pooch?"

Dash growled deeper in his throat. The fur along his backbone stood up. Mitsi had never seen him act like this.

The other soldier laughed. "He's quite the watchdog. For a dust mop." They turned back to their job, working their way down the street, away from Mitsi and Dash.

Mitsi stepped closer to read the sign they'd posted. INSTRUCTIONS TO ALL PERSONS OF JAPANESE ANCESTRY was printed right at the top, in dark, stern letters. Persons of Japanese ancestry?

She scooped Dash up and ran inside the drugstore, even though dogs weren't allowed. "You have to come. Now."

Ted read the first paragraph out loud, his face turning as white as vanilla ice cream.

"What does 'evacuated' mean?" Mitsi asked.

Ted clenched his fists. "They're making us leave."

"Who is?" Mitsi's legs wouldn't hold her up anymore. Leave? Where would they go? She plunked down on the sidewalk, still holding Dash.

"They." Ted slapped the paper. "The government. Everyone."

Mitsi started to tremble, tasting chocolate syrup at the back of her throat. She thought she might upchuck right there.

"We've got to get home. Pronto." Ted yanked Dash's leash out of her hand. "Come on."

He and Dash started to run, but Mitsi couldn't move. Dash dug in his paws, scrambling away from Ted, barking for Mitsi to come.

At the racket, Ted turned. When he saw her frozen on the sidewalk, he ran back. "It'll be okay." The look in his eyes said the opposite. "But we gotta go." He yanked her up.

Mitsi began to move, trying her best to keep up with Ted's long legs. She stumbled a few times. But she kept moving.

And tried hard not to think about that look in her brother's eyes.

CHAPTER FIVE

Dear General DeWitt

Mom sorted through the storage closet under the stairs. "Only one week." She froze, like a wind-up doll with a broken spring. "How can we be ready to leave in one week?"

Pop patted her on the back. "It won't be for long, Junko. Not for long."

Mitsi had never heard her father tell a lie before. No one knew how long they would be gone. There were lots of guesses. Maybe two weeks. Maybe two years. Maybe forever. She went to her room and stomach-flopped on her bed. She was supposed to be sorting her belongings into boxes: take, give away, sell. Mitsi lifted her head up and looked around the room she'd slept in ever since she'd been born. Then she flopped back down, burying her face in her pillow. Why couldn't there be a box that said stay?

Mom peeked her head into Mitsi's room. "How's

it going in here?" She frowned. "Mitsi. We don't have much time."

Mitsi rolled around Dash and off the bed. She picked up an old doll and tossed it in the giveaway box. "I'm doing the best I can," she said.

Mom held up a jump rope with a broken handle. "This looks like it could get tossed."

"But —" Judy had given her that jump rope. For her seventh birthday. Back when they did birthdays together. Back when they were Betsy, Tacy, and Tib. Mitsi swallowed hard. "Sure. Throw it away." She eased back to her bed, hugging her knees to her chest. Dash licked her ear.

Mom nudged Dash out of the way and sat down next to Mitsi. She reached for Chubby Bear, joggled him back and forth, and began to sing: *"You are my sunshine, my only sunshine. You make me happy when skies are gray."*

When Mitsi was little, Chubby Bear would "sing" that song every night. Even when she got older and figured out that stuffed teddy bears really can't sing, whenever Mom sang "You Are My Sunshine" in her Chubby Bear voice, Mitsi felt happy. Safe.

Mitsi took Chubby Bear from her mother. "I'm too big for stuffed animals." She tossed him toward the giveaway box. Dash jumped, moving to his hiding spot under the desk.

Pop called out, "Junko? What about the toaster?"

"Guess we'd better get back to work." Mom glanced around the room. "Pop's leaving soon with a load for the church. If there's anything you want him to take, better get it now." Pastor Andrews had marked the floor of the church gymnasium into big squares. Each family got one square for storage. Pop had already taken over one carton, filled with a jumble of teacups and kimonos and family photos. As Mom passed the giveaway box, she reached for Chubby Bear. "Let's hang on to this guy." She tossed him back to Mitsi.

Mitsi set Chubby Bear aside. Each person could take only what they could carry. Pop had new muscles from working at Uncle Shig's. He would haul the two big suitcases, one filled with his things and sheets and blankets, the other with dishes and silverware. Mom would carry two smaller bags: hers and Obaachan's. Ted and Mitsi each got one suitcase and a book bag.

Mitsi bent under the desk to rub Dash's ears. "I wish I could hide, too." She got to work, sorting through eleven years of stuff. A baby doll with chopped-off hair, the stamp collection she'd started in second grade, and a pair of roller skates went in the giveaway box.

She picked up her scrapbook. What about that? She opened it up.

There she was at age three, in an outfit that made her look like a gumdrop. How could Mom have dressed her like that? Another page turn and there it was. Mitsi's sixth birthday. The first time Mags had ever said, "Let's make a Mitsi sandwich!" The three girls scrunched close together, with Mitsi smack-dab in the middle. Pop had grabbed his Kodak and snapped them, laughing, forever friends.

Most of the pages held memories shared with Mags and Judy. They'd caught the chicken pox at the same time; there was a photo of them comparing who got the most spots. Somehow they'd all made it into the All-City Spelling Bee in third grade. Judy was the best speller, but she'd lost in the final round by spelling "philosophy" with "ie" instead of a "y." Mitsi and Mags went out in the second round. She couldn't remember which words tripped them up. But she remembered Mags's father taking them out for Frango mint sundaes at Frederick & Nelson afterward.

Mitsi skipped ahead to a photo from her birthday last year. The three of them had gotten permission to ride downtown on the bus all by themselves. They'd seen *The Sea Hawk*. Over hamburgers afterward, they'd argued about whether it would be better to be a pirate like Geoffrey Thorpe, played by the dashing Errol Flynn, or a princess like Doña Maria, played by the glamorous Brenda Marshall. Judy voted for princess; Mitsi and Mags leaned toward pirates. That had been one of Mitsi's best-ever birthdays.

She closed the scrapbook, running her fingers over the cover. It was hard to believe all that fun and friendship was over. But it seemed to be. She should probably just throw the darned thing away. Mags and Judy had certainly thrown *her* away. But she couldn't bring herself to dump the scrapbook in the garbage.

All this deciding gave her a headache. She wandered into Ted's room to see what he was doing.

Dash padded along. Ted's suitcase lay open on the bed. He'd packed a bag of marbles, a baseball glove, and magic tricks. And not much else.

"Are you taking your entire magic collection?" It sure looked like it.

Ted shrugged. "I gave a bunch of tricks to the YMCA. For the summer day camp."

That was where Ted first learned to do magic. "Remember how you got me with the magnetic pencil trick?" Mitsi asked. He'd come home from camp the first day and performed it for her. She'd really believed that a plain old pencil could stick to his hand magnetically. When he'd shown her how it was done, she'd felt like a big goof.

Ted grinned. "I get you with *every* trick." He shuffled things around in his suitcase, trying to make room for a football. "Maybe if I took out some socks." He held a couple pairs in each hand.

"I won't tell." Mitsi went back to her own room but still couldn't face the piles. She decided to pack for Dash. That would be easy. He didn't have much. She put his yellow ball, his blue blanket, and his dinner bowl in her book bag. Then she got the box of Milk-Bones from the kitchen.

"Where are you going with that?" Pop tied string around a box marked KASHINO.

"Don't worry — I'll carry it." Pop had enough to tote.

"Honey." Pop cleared his throat. "Dash can't go with us."

"What?" Mitsi held the Milk-Bones close to her chest, like a shield. "What are you talking about?"

Pop rubbed his eyes. "No pets." His voice was froggy, as if he had a bad cold. "That's one of the rules."

"NO!" The word exploded out of Mitsi so loud that Mom came running.

"Is everything okay?" Mom asked.

Mitsi turned to her. "Dash is like your third kid. That's what you always say!"

"Oh, honey." Mom rubbed her hands up and down her arms so hard and fast, Mitsi thought they might catch on fire. "In the eyes of General DeWitt, he's a pet."

"Who's General DeWitt?" Mitsi tugged on Mom's hands to get her to stop rubbing. She didn't want anything worse to happen.

"The man in charge of the evacuation," Pop said.

"But Dash has his own Christmas stocking!" Mitsi's head felt like it might pop off her neck and bob up into the air like a helium-filled balloon. "They can't do this to us. To me."

Mom reached for her, but Mitsi jerked away, her hands pressing, pressing, pressing on her head.

"We are all leaving something behind," Pop pointed out. Last night, they had sold Mom's Singer Featherweight sewing machine for five dollars. *Five* dollars. And tomorrow, Mr. Adams from Pop's old work was coming to buy their car.

"Dash is not a *thing*." Mitsi mumbled the words to her shoes.

"We'll find a good home for him." Mom stopped rubbing her arms and held them out. Mitsi leaned in. "A temporary home."

"*Shikata ga nai*," said Obaachan. She tied another box shut.

Mitsi was so sick of hearing those words. She breathed deeply, taking in the starchy smell of Mom's clean apron, the talcum powder from her bath. It cannot be helped? It cannot be helped? Couldn't some things be helped?

Mom patted Mitsi's back. "It'll be okay, honey."

She kissed the top of her head. "Now, I really need you to work on packing."

. . .

Miss Wyatt opened *Little House in the Big Woods* and began to read. "'Once upon a time, sixty years ago, a little girl lived in the Big Woods of Wisconsin, in a little gray house made of logs.'"

All year, Mitsi had loved listening to Miss Wyatt read aloud. She was as good as a movie star, using different voices, reading the exciting parts really fast and the sad parts slow and solemn. But today, Mitsi did everything she could to block out the story. She needed all of her energy to think about Dash. To figure out how to keep him with the family. Miss Wyatt encouraged them to doodle while she read, and the page under Mitsi's pencil was covered with paw prints and big brown doggy eyes. She was shading in Dash's nose when she realized Miss Wyatt's voice had changed again.

"I think we'll stop there for now." Miss Wyatt took in the class with a serious expression. "Laura Ingalls Wilder wrote simply, but from her heart. And her words have had a lasting impact on many,

many people." She carefully set the book on her desk. "As you know, some of our friends will be leaving us soon."

Mitsi felt her cheeks flare red-hot. She stopped drawing.

"We all have feelings about this. And it's good for us to put such feelings into words. I'd like each of you to write a letter, expressing your thoughts about, about . . ." Miss Wyatt paused, pressing a flowered hanky to her nose. She was quiet for so long, Mitsi glanced up, wondering if she'd forgotten what she was going to say. "About this sad time for our school." She cleared her throat. "It can be a paragraph or a page, but it should be from the heart. Yes, Roy?"

"What about them?" Roy tipped his head toward Kenji. "Do they write letters, too?"

Miss Wyatt's mouth turned into a straight line. Roy shrunk back in his chair at the look she gave him. "This is a class project." Their sweet teacher's voice was cold. Measured. "And *everyone* sitting in this room is a part of our class." Miss Wyatt reached toward the pencil holder on her desk. "Who needs a writing utensil?" Not one student raised a hand.

Mitsi picked up her pencil again. The last thing she felt like doing was writing a letter, but she didn't want to disappoint Miss Wyatt. On the top line of her paper, she wrote the word "dear."

Dear who? *Dear Judy and Mags?* Then what? *I'm sad we aren't friends?* Maybe *Dear Hudson, Thank you for the valentine card, even though you forgot to sign it?* Mitsi chewed on the pencil eraser. How about: *Dear Patty, You look really ugly when you make slanty eyes.*

Those words would be from the heart, but Mitsi didn't think they were what Miss Wyatt had in mind.

She wiggled her pencil tip over the paper. She could write to her teacher. Something like *Dear Miss Wyatt, Thank you for teaching us to be good citizens. I wish being a good citizen canceled out having black hair and a Japanese name.*

Mitsi made a little doodle in the upper left-hand corner of her paper. It looked like the doodles she'd been making while Miss Wyatt had been reading. Dog doodles. Dash doodles.

She sat up in her desk. Miss Wyatt said it was good to put your feelings into words. And right there, over the blackboard, was a poster that said THE PEN IS MIGHTIER THAN THE SWORD.

Mitsi knew what to do. She wrote slowly, precisely, using her best penmanship.

> *Dear General DeWitt,*
>
> *My family and I have followed every single rule. I have to leave my house and the bed I've slept in since I was a baby. We have to leave our car and sewing machine and even my grandmother's antique dolls. But Mom says these are only "things" and what matters most is that our family will be together. My dog Dash is not a thing. He is a part of our family. I am pretty strong, for a girl. I can carry a suitcase in one hand and Dash in the other.*
>
> *Please do not make us leave him, too.*
>
> *Sincerely yours,*
>
> *Mitsue Kashino*

At the bottom of the letter, she drew her best-ever picture of Dash. She captured his perky ears, and the way the fur fell like bangs over his brown eyes. She could almost feel his cold, wet nose!

When the recess bell rang, Mitsi filed out behind her classmates, but she didn't add her letter to the growing pile on the teacher's desk.

• • •

When she got home from school, Mom helped her find General DeWitt's address and gave her a three-cent stamp. "Don't be disappointed if he doesn't answer, Mitsi." Her voice was soft and sad. "He has so many things to do."

"I won't be disappointed." Mitsi licked the stamp and pasted it on the envelope. "I know he will answer me."

And she was right.

CHAPTER SIX

Stay, Dash, Stay

The buzzing stopped as soon as Mitsi stepped into the cloakroom to hang up her coat. Her class-mates were suddenly intent on placing their lunch boxes just so in their cubbies, on hanging their own coats and jackets up neatly, carefully avoiding eye contact with her, and Grace, and Kenji. Patty was quiet, too. Didn't even make slanty eyes. It had been all over the newspaper. Everyone knew these were their last days at school.

"Shall we pick up where we left off in *Little House in the Big Woods*?" Miss Wyatt opened the book. "'In the winter,'" she read, "'the cream was not as yellow as it was in the summer and the butter churned in it was white and not as pretty. Ma liked everything on her table to be pretty, so in the wintertime she colored the butter.'"

Mitsi drew a funny picture of a cow as she listened. Mom did that sometimes when she bought

71

margarine to save money — mixing in yellow food coloring so it looked like butter. As she drew, Mitsi wondered why Miss Wyatt had selected *this* book to read aloud. Most every fifth-grade girl had read it ages ago. Mitsi remembered the first time she'd read it and how relieved she was at the end that Pa didn't kill the deer he was hunting, because he thought it was so beautiful.

The sisters in the story, Laura and Mary, lived far away from other people and didn't have any friends but each other. And Ma and Pa. Mitsi hoped she wouldn't be as lonely in the camp because her family — her whole family — would be together.

Mitsi folded her arms on her desk and rested her head there, thinking about her letter to General DeWitt. She should have mentioned that Dash was very friendly. That he'd never hurt a soul. And that he wouldn't take up much room. She should have told him that Dash was trained and didn't bark, except at the mailman.

When the recess bell rang, Grace asked if Mitsi wanted to play jacks. "Sure." Mitsi shrugged. "I guess."

They set up their game on the far side of the play

yard, away from the other kids. They flipped to see who'd go first. Grace won.

"I hope we're at the same camp." Grace tossed her jacks.

"Me, too," Mitsi said, though she wasn't sure. Grace was bossy. And she didn't like books.

Grace scooped up a jack with her right hand and let the ball bounce again, flipping the caught jack to her left hand.

"I went to camp once," Grace continued. "Church camp. We roasted marshmallows and went canoeing and did arts and crafts. I made a lanyard."

Mitsi nodded politely.

"So do you think this camp will be like that?" Grace looked at Mitsi, letting the ball bounce twice.

Mitsi didn't want to talk about the camp anymore. She didn't even want to play jacks. She wanted to go over to the swings and sit on the one between Judy and Mags like she used to. The swing Patty was in. And she wanted to race with her friends, pumping their legs hard, to see who could get the highest. She wouldn't care if she lost. She just wanted to be over there, soaring through the air with her best friends.

"Do you?" Grace asked again. The bell saved Mitsi from having to answer.

While they were in line to go back into the classroom, Kenji tapped Mitsi on the shoulder. "Me and Grace are leaving tomorrow," he said. "Are you?"

She shook her head. "No. Friday." Instead of hanging paper cones of flowers on her neighbors' doorknobs on May Day morning, she'd be on a bus, heading to Camp Harmony.

"What are you going to do about Dash?" he asked.

"What do you mean?" Mags butted in. "What's wrong with Dash?"

Mitsi didn't answer her. Why should she? "I wrote a letter," she told Kenji. "Maybe they'll let me take him."

Kenji gave her a hopeful smile. "You're a good writer," he said. "Maybe they will."

• • •

Mitsi thought about Kenji and Grace as she walked to school the next morning. They were on their way to Camp Harmony, or maybe Pinedale, at that very moment. She wondered what they were feeling. Maybe scared — even Grace. Mitsi sure was.

The camps sounded like big places. Pop said there'd be nearly ten thousand people at Camp Harmony alone. She might not even see Kenji or Grace if they were there. Might not see them ever again.

She was thinking so hard about Kenji and Grace, and about going to camp, that she thought she was dreaming when she reached the meet-up bench and saw someone there.

"I thought I might have missed you." Mags held out an envelope with Mitsi's name written in that big loopy penmanship on the front. "This is for you. It's the letter I wrote in class."

Mitsi didn't reach for it. "How come you didn't disguise your handwriting this time?"

"This time?" Mags looked genuinely puzzled. Mitsi never realized what a good actress she was. Then Mags's face changed. She knew that Mitsi knew.

"You can keep that one." Mitsi started walking again.

"Mitsi!" Mags called after her. "Please wait."

But Mitsi didn't wait. And Mags didn't try to catch up.

• • •

It was a day for envelopes. Another one sat in the middle of the kitchen table when Mitsi got home from school. Pop was still at Uncle Shig's, and Mom was helping Mrs. Iseri. Only Obaachan was home.

"Tea," she announced, reaching for her special tin. Mitsi sat at the kitchen table, turning the envelope around and around. Dash plunked himself at her feet, sniffing hopefully from time to time. Finally, the kettle whistled and the tea was steeped and ready to drink. Obaachan served it in the gold-rimmed teacups she'd bought with Green Stamps. After they'd both had a sip, Obaachan patted Mitsi's hand. "Now read."

For a moment, Mitsi wondered if she should wait for Mom and Pop. But she had to know General DeWitt's answer. She ripped open the envelope.

The paper inside was fancy, but the words weren't.

Dear Miss Kashino:
   We all must make sacrifices in times of war. I regret that we cannot allow pets in the camps.
   Yours very truly,
   General John L. DeWitt

"It's not fair!" Mitsi threw the letter on the floor. Dash whined, pawing at her legs so she'd pull him up on her lap. A tear dripped on the table. Mitsi wiped it away, then pushed at Dash's legs. Pushed him away. "Down." It wasn't his fault, but she was mad. Too mad to be nice to anyone, even Dash. Another tear dripped on her leg.

"You are a brave girl," said Obaachan. "To write a general!" She patted Mitsi's hand. "Brave, brave girl."

Mitsi didn't feel one bit brave. She felt used up and dry like an old piece of bubble gum. Dash whined. She scooted the chair back and patted her lap. "Come on, Dash. I'm sorry."

He jumped up and she squeezed him close, his wispy fur brushing her cheek as he nibbled her ear. She squeezed him even tighter. He was her best friend. Really her only friend. How was she ever going to let him go? And who would take care of him until she could get back? Those questions pricked at her heart until it was a flat tire, ka-thumping in her chest.

Mom and Pop were as sad as she was about the letter. Ted kicked the door frame. "We'll find him a good home," Mom promised.

"Not a home!" Mitsi cried. "Just a place to stay."

Mom made a dozen telephone calls. But no one could take a dog.

"We'll try again tomorrow," Pop said as he tucked Mitsi into bed.

"Tomorrow's the only day we have!" Mitsi fingered the frayed hem of her blanket. "What if we don't find a place?"

"We will." Pop kissed her forehead. "We will. Now try to get some sleep."

Dash started out on the floor, at the foot of Mitsi's bed, as always. But after a while, he hopped up next to her. Mitsi wrapped him in a hug. When he fell asleep and began to twitch in his dreams, she rested her hand on his side. "Good dog," she whispered. "Good dog." He relaxed.

"We'll find something," she said. "With someone who really loves dogs." As she said those words, a tiny idea popped into her head. An idea so perfect that it was hard to fall asleep. But, finally, with Dash snoring next to her, she did.

First thing in the morning, Mitsi ran through the neighborhood, to the house with the white picket fence. She unlatched the gate, hurrying up to the front door. Mrs. Bowker answered her knocking, and invited her inside right away when Mitsi told her about the letter.

"I am so proud of you for trying," Mrs. Bowker said. "And so sorry the general said no."

Mitsi thought she had cried out all her tears, but a couple more leaked out. "Mom says it might be for the best. What if people *could* bring pets, and someone brought a dog that didn't like Dash? What if they got into a fight and Dash got hurt?" Mitsi rubbed her nose.

"Oh, my lands, yes. That would be bad." A tear leaked out of Mrs. Bowker's eye, too. "Very bad."

They sat together in the warm, messy kitchen that smelled of cinnamon and those other good things Mitsi never could identify.

Mom had said it was too much to ask. Pop agreed. But Mitsi had to. She studied the black and white squares on Mrs. Bowker's kitchen floor. There was no other choice except Uncle Shig's neighbor, who didn't like dogs one bit. Not even a fluff of love like Dash.

Mitsi took a deep breath. "I was wondering if you could keep Dash. Only for a little while." That last part was sort of a fib. Nobody had any idea how long they'd be gone. But Mitsi *hoped* it wouldn't be long.

She glued her eyes to the tabletop. The room percolated with all kinds of noises she hadn't noticed earlier: the coffee pot gurgling on the stove, the soft hiss of the lightbulb overhead, a creak from under her feet.

"Mitsi." Mrs. Bowker cleared her throat.

Mitsi squeezed her eyes closed. She squeezed her fingers together, too, in a prayer.

Mrs. Bowker said her name again. And then Mitsi felt a warm hand on top of her two hands. Mitsi opened her eyes. She looked up.

"I would be honored to take care of Dash. Thank you for asking me." Mrs. Bowker sat back in her chair and held her arms open. Mitsi flew into the hug and started crying all over again. When they were both pretty soggy, Mitsi reached into her dungarees pocket and pulled out a small wad of dollar bills. "This is to help pay for his food."

Mrs. Bowker looked at the money. "Tell you what," she said. "How about if we trade dog food for work? My knees aren't getting any younger and I'm going to need lots of help in the garden."

"Mom said I had to, if you said yes." Mitsi held out the money again. "Besides, what if we're gone for, for longer than we think?"

"I'll keep careful track. I promise," said Mrs. Bowker. "And I'll make you work off every penny I spend on Dash. Is that a deal?"

"Are you sure?"

"I'm sure."

• • •

That night, Mitsi held Dash's leash in one hand and pulled her wagon with the other. It was loaded up with a blanket and toys and dog dishes and food. A flat of strawberry plants for Mrs. Bowker's garden teetered on top of everything else. Pop had brought them from Uncle Shig's. Mitsi moved slowly, partly so nothing would fall out. But mostly because she wanted this walk to last as long as possible.

Mrs. Bowker asked for help getting Dash settled in. "Should we put his bed by the stove?" she asked.

"Well, it would be warm there," Mitsi answered. She couldn't expect Mrs. Bowker to let Dash sleep in her bedroom. But she hated to think of him by himself. Especially tonight.

"Where does he sleep at your house?" Mrs. Bowker asked.

Mitsi decided to be honest. "In my room. On the floor, at the foot of the bed."

"Well then, that's where he'll sleep here." Mrs. Bowker put Dash's bed in her room. At the foot of her bed.

"Sometimes he sleeps with me," Mitsi confessed. Would that make her change her mind?

Mrs. Bowker looked a bit surprised. "Does he snore?"

"Sometimes." Mitsi held her breath.

Mrs. Bowker smiled. "Well, so did my husband. It'll be like old times."

Mitsi let her breath out again. It was going to be fine. Dash was going to be fine. She hid his yellow ball in the magazine rack for a morning game of hide-and-seek. She put the bag of kibble and the box of Milk-Bones in Mrs. Bowker's pantry.

"Here's the last thing." Mitsi held out Dash's leash.

"Not quite." Mrs. Bowker took out her Brownie camera.

Mitsi wrapped her arms around Dash. She inhaled as deeply as she could so she wouldn't forget his smell.

Mrs. Bowker held the camera up to her eye, peering through the viewfinder. "Say 'cheese.'"

It was a good thing it was only a camera, not an X-ray machine, or all Mrs. Bowker would see was Mitsi's heart, broken into a billion kibble-size bits.

CHAPTER SEVEN

Camp Harmony

Her room echoed. Mitsi felt like she was sleeping in a gymnasium. Or a cemetery. All the furniture, including the beds, was gone, so they were sleeping on the floor, wrapped up in blankets. She snugged the blankets tighter around her and reached for Dash. But when her arms only gathered up air, she picked up her makeshift bed and carried it from her bedroom to the front room with Mom and Pop. Under the blanket of their breathing, she was finally able to go to sleep.

They got up in the dark morning hours, like they used to when they went fishing at Point No Point on Uncle Shig's boat. Mitsi couldn't stop yawning as she buttoned her blouse. Pop toasted bread on a fork over the stove and they spread it with the last of the homemade strawberry jam. After Mitsi and Ted drained their glasses of milk, Mom washed and dried them and carefully added them to Pop's big suitcase. She did the same with the grown-ups' coffee mugs, but she left the percolator on the stove top. No room in any of the bags for that.

When she was ready to go, Mitsi sat on the front steps, Chubby Bear under one arm, playing with the cardboard tag pinned to her coat. She'd worn a tag like this when she'd gone off to kindergarten. *That* tag had said MY NAME IS MITSI KASHINO. I AM IN MISS STEAD'S CLASS. It was a friendly tag. Not like this one. This one had a number on it. That was all. Number 11817. The same number was pinned on Pop's coat, Mom's coat, Ted's, and even Obaachan's. It was their family number. No Kashino family. Just 11817.

Mr. Adams pulled into their driveway. In their car. He'd offered to take them to the assembly point. "He said it was the least he could do," Mitsi overheard Pop tell Mom. "He feels real bad about the whole thing."

"He's a good man," Mom had said, which was true. Even so, it was hard to see him behind the wheel, where Pop should be sitting.

Mr. Adams jumped out of the car. "Let me help you, Junko." He took the brown suitcase from Mom.

"Thank you." She gripped the house key tight in her other hand.

"Time to go." Pop took one step off the porch. "Time to say good-bye."

The light from the rising sun caught Mom's face as she glanced over at Pop. Mitsi remembered the time when she was about three and had seen a photo from Mom's high school graduation. "That's my mommy," she'd told Obaachan. "She's so pretty."

Mom was pretty. As beautiful as that actress that played Scarlett O'Hara in *Gone with the Wind*. And as brave, too. Now Mom smiled at Pop. "Not good-bye. See you later. Right?"

Pop nodded.

Mitsi couldn't watch her mother slide the key into the lock. How many times had she turned that big brass knob after school, eager to ask permission to go over to Judy or Mags's house? How many times had she run down those seven steps to greet Pop when he'd come home from work? How many times had Dash been waiting on the other side of that door, his tail wagging sixty miles a minute, as if Mitsi were the best thing he'd ever seen in his whole doggy life, better even than a T-bone steak?

With that final *click* of the lock, Mitsi felt as though they were shutting the door to a life they'd never know again.

"It's okay, Mits." Ted handed her a hanky. She hadn't realized she was crying. "I've got a new trick I'm going to show you on our way to camp."

Mitsi blew her nose. Ted could saw a lady in half and then conjure up a rhino wearing a polka-dot swimsuit, but that still wouldn't take her mind off their lonely, empty house. Or Dash.

"That's it, then." Mom dropped the house keys into her pocketbook with a clunk, not a jingle. She took Obaachan's arm. "Come, Mother."

Mr. Adams closed the trunk and hurried around to open the door for them. Ted and Mitsi squeezed into the backseat with Mom and Obaachan. Pop sat up front with Mr. Adams, who drove slowly down the street, both hands tight on the steering wheel.

Mrs. Bowker stood in her yard, holding Dash, waving his paw at them as they passed. "Good-bye," she called. "God bless."

Mr. Adams honk-honked the horn. Mitsi pressed the flat of her hand to the glass. Her voice didn't work to call out good-bye in return. She pivoted away from the window and leaned against the seat.

She had spent hours tracing the little corded edges that divided this very seat into thirds. She'd often pretended she was helping Pop steer by turning the knob on the handle that rolled the window up and down. This car had taken them for picnics to Alki Beach and to pick strawberries at Uncle Shig's farm in Bellevue. It had even taken Mitsi to the hospital when she'd had her tonsils out. And she couldn't forget all the hours snuggled up against Obaachan, dreaming away the long drive to visit Auntie Nobuko and Uncle Hiroshi in Spokane. Those had all been good rides in Pop's car.

This was not a good ride. It wasn't even Pop's car anymore; that's what Pop said when Mr. Adams offered to let him drive. Today, they were going someplace worse than the doctor's office. Mitsi's arm still ached from the shots she'd had to get. She didn't even know what they all were for. Her whole family had waited in a long line that snaked up Main Street and into Dr. Suzuki's office.

"I don't even think you'd need this many shots if you were going to the tropics," one man in line had grumbled. "What kind of place are they send-ing us to?"

"Camp Harmony." Another man spit on the street. "What a joke. There's no harmony there. I heard people are sleeping in horse stalls." He started to say something else, but his wife gave him the stink eye.

"Little pitchers, big ears," she said.

The man nodded, scratching the back of his neck. He smiled at Mitsi but didn't say anything more.

Mitsi had thought Camp Harmony couldn't be too bad if there were horses. But at Judy's horse camp, she'd slept with the other campers, not her horse. This man probably didn't know what he was talking about. Mitsi had passed the rest of the time waiting in the long line, woolgathering about the kind of horse *she'd* like to ride. Not a black one, like Judy's. A palomino — yes, that's what she'd ride. She daydreamed about Quicksilver — that's what she'd name him — until Dr. Suzuki's nurse jabbed her in the arm. Three times. Same arm. Lucky for her, it was her left.

She rubbed her sore arm now and turned back to the window, spotted with raindrops. The drops tumbled down the glass, crisscrossing each other to form a blurry screen. But Mitsi could still see every empty storefront. A padlocked chain bolted shut the front doors at Higo. A pair of two-by-fours were nailed in an X across the entrance to Cheeky's café. Nearly every store in Nihonmachi was closed.

The rain came down harder. Mr. Adams switched on the wipers. *Good riddance. Good riddance. Good riddance*, they taunted as they swept back and forth across the windshield.

At the corner of 8th and Lane, Mr. Adams braked to a stop and killed the engine. Soldiers in olive drab uniforms patrolled back and forth. Carrying guns. Calling out orders. Shivering, Mitsi grabbed Ted's coat sleeve. Mr. Adams and Pop unloaded the trunk. After the last bag was out, Mr. Adams offered his hand. "Good luck to you, Kash." They shook and then Pop picked up his two suitcases. Mr. Adams fumbled a white handkerchief from his pocket and wiped his eyes. "I wish —"

Pop nodded. "I know. I know." Then he picked up the two biggest suitcases. "Thank you for the ride." He walked into the crowd.

Mitsi slung her book bag over her shoulder and grabbed her own suitcase, keeping a grip on Ted with her free hand. She tried to walk around the puddles, but there were too many. Her anklets got soaked. She and Ted followed Pop and Mom and Obaachan past this clump of people, around that family, until they reached a soldier with a clipboard.

"Kashino," said Pop. "11817."

"Okay." The soldier made a check mark on the paper and then looked around. He pointed. "That's your truck over there, folks. Fifth one down."

A mountain range of soggy luggage stretched alongside the line of trucks. Mitsi couldn't see where it ended. And the people! It was like when the salmon ran through the Ballard Locks, trying to get upstream to spawn — a writhing, rolling wall of motion. Mitsi heard snippets of Japanese and hepcat slang. Mothers scolded their children for splashing in mud puddles, and teenage boys bantered back and forth. Two little boys had found sticks and were shooting at each other. *"Pow-pow, pow, pow, pow."*

Mitsi dragged herself along behind her family, all of them getting wetter and wetter. It took forever to move a few feet. Off to the side, two girls were hugging good-bye: one blonde head, one black. Mitsi glanced around. There were quite a few white faces. Neighbors. Friends.

"Mitsi, Mitsi!" A lady waved a lacy handkerchief. "Dear, over here!"

Mom nodded, and Mitsi hurried over to Miss Wyatt. "I couldn't let you leave without something to remember us by." Her teacher pressed a package into Mitsi's hands. "Good luck, Mitsi. You'll be in my prayers."

Mitsi watched Miss Wyatt weave her way through the throngs. Had she come to see Kenji and Grace off, too? Had she brought them gifts? Mitsi tucked the package under her coat so it wouldn't get wet, then made her way back to where Mom waited, sharing an umbrella with Mrs. Iseri. Mitsi ducked under it, too, to open her package.

"Paper!" Mitsi exclaimed. "And colored pencils." The drawing pad was the perfect size to carry around. The pencils were travel-size, too. Just like real artists might take when they went outdoors to sketch. Miss Wyatt had written her address on the back of the drawing pad.

"That was sure nice of Miss Wyatt," Mom said.

"She is *yasashii hito*." Obaachan patted her heart.

Mitsi nodded. Miss Wyatt *was* a kind person. Would the teachers where they were going be as nice? Would there even be teachers? School? Nobody seemed to know the answers to these questions.

The line continued to move a few slow steps at a time. Mitsi's hair ribbons melted into soggy pink spaghetti noodles. She heard someone say it was nine thirty, but it felt like they'd been waiting for days, not hours. Step after step, they shuffled ahead and then it was their turn to climb into the big green Army truck. Pop lifted her up over the truck gate and some stranger helped her onto a long wooden bench. Mitsi sat down, tucking her suitcase under the bench. She squeezed Chubby Bear close to her chest, pretending he was Dash. If she kept her eyes closed very tight, she could still smell his fur.

After a while, the truck's engine grumbled to life. The truck lurched forward and then they were bouncing along. Nobody said anything. It was impossible to talk over the engine noise, anyway.

Somewhere along the way, Mitsi fell asleep on Ted's shoulder. The next thing she knew, two hours had passed, and Ted was shaking her awake from a good dream about playing fetch with Dash in Mrs. Bowker's garden. "Mits, we're here."

She opened her eyes, still sleepy. For a moment, she was confused. Where were the tulips and the daffodils? Where was Dash? Then she remembered.

The truck growled through a big gate in the barbed wire fence and pulled to a stop at a sentry box. Soldiers with guns and stern faces checked out the truck before giving the okay for it to roll inside. Mitsi caught a glimpse of the guard tower, high above, and the glint of gun barrels up there, too.

And then, she saw something that made her wonder if she was still dreaming. Beyond the guard tower stood a Ferris wheel. She tapped Ted's arm, pointing.

"Yeah. Don't you remember? This is where they hold the state fair." He shifted his suitcase to his other hand. "I rode that once. You were too little."

Mitsi vaguely remembered a trip to the fair. "We had scones. Raspberry scones."

Ted nodded. "And burgers with fried onions."

The wind rocked the painted seats, but the wheel itself was completely still. It looked as if it was leaning away from the commotion, embarrassed by what was going on below.

"Over here." Ted led the way to the end of a line so long Mitsi thought it must stretch clear back to Seattle. Mitsi hung on to Mom's coat hem. She didn't care if she looked like a baby. People were wandering around like Bo Peep's sheep; she certainly didn't want to get herded in the wrong direction. If she lost sight of her family, she might never find them again. There were so many people and so many faces she didn't recognize.

In front of them, a mom held a baby in one arm and a suitcase in the other. A little boy — maybe two years old — clutched one end of a ribbon tied to the suitcase handle.

After they'd been standing in the line for quite a while, the little boy started to whine. "I want to go home." He plopped down. Right in the mud.

"Davy!" His mother tugged at him. "Get up. Now!"

Davy kicked his feet, ignoring his mother and splashing Mitsi.

"Oh, I'm so sorry." The mother apologized.

Mitsi brushed off her legs. "It's okay."

Ted bent over, eye level with the little kid. "Hey, wanna see a magic trick?" He pulled a quarter out of his pocket.

Davy grabbed for it.

Ted tossed the quarter in the air. "Stand up, and I'll show you."

Davy stood, oblivious to the muddy stain on his rear. "Show you," he mimicked.

For the next hour, while the line moved one inch at a time, Ted kept Davy entertained. Finally, he and his mother reached the front of the line. Ted pulled the coin from Davy's ear, then handed it to him.

"What do you say?" His mother nudged him.

"Thank you." Davy looked like he'd been given his own cowboy set, complete with pony.

"I thank you, too." The lady set down her suitcase and put out her hand. "I'm Helen Tokuda. You've met Davy." She jiggled the sleeping baby in her arms. "This is Donna."

Mom and Pop introduced themselves. "Perhaps we'll be near one another," Mom said.

Mrs. Tokuda blinked hard. "That would be wonderful."

"This way, ma'am." A soldier waved her forward and she tugged Davy inside the reception room.

"The poor thing," Mom said. "Two children and all by herself." She hugged Ted. "You were great with that little boy."

"Step up, sir." Another soldier motioned Pop into the reception room. The rest of the family hung back. Obaachan nodded to some older ladies about her age. Ted started up a conversation with a goofy-looking teenager. Mom chewed on her cuticle. Mitsi held tight to her belongings, trying not to get knocked over by the noise and confusion.

When Pop returned, he said they'd been assigned to Area A. "Barracks 52," he said.

"Where did that nice Mrs. Tokuda end up?" Mom asked. "I know she could use some help."

Pop shook his head. "It's a madhouse in there. I lost sight of her." He picked up the two big suitcases. "But we'll keep an eye out."

Mom picked up her bags, too. Obaachan didn't even try to use her cane on the muddy pathways. She took small, careful steps. So Pop took small, careful steps. Like a family of turtles, they followed as he led them away from the main gate, deeper into

Area A. They plodded along oozy aisles between rows and rows and rows of slapped-together barracks, all long rectangles like a kids' building set. Mitsi had no idea how Pop knew where he was going. She was certain they were lost. She stopped and looked around.

"There it is. 52." Mitsi pointed at their new "apartment." Compared to this building, the sheds on Uncle Shig's farm looked like mansions.

"Home sweet home." Mom pulled the door open and stepped inside.

They squeezed in behind her. Five Army cots were lined up in the middle of a space smaller than their kitchen at home.

There were no mattresses or pillows or blankets on the cots. Just some cotton bags. Except for a stove for heat, the cots were the only furnishings. No table. No chairs. No nothing.

"We're going to have to climb over each other to get to bed." Ted dropped his bags with a thump.

Flimsy plywood walls separated their room from the one next door. They could hear everything. A woman was crying.

"At least it's not a horse barn," a man's voice said. "That's where the Akis ended up."

The woman sobbed even louder.

"Well." Mom set down her bags, taking in the layer of sawdust and grime. "We'd better find a broom."

Mitsi agreed with the lady next door. This might not be a horse stall, but it still smelled of them. And not the good part of horses, either.

"Not just a broom." Obaachan pinched her nose between her fingers. "Bleach. Rags."

Pop tucked his suitcases in the corner. He gathered the cotton bags from the cots. "And some hay to fill these."

Mitsi stared. They were going to sleep on hay? Like animals?

Mom straightened her hat. "Ted, you watch Mitsi while we find some supplies." The three adults headed out, leaving Mitsi and Ted alone in their new home.

The lady next door bawled even louder.

"Pull up a seat." Ted patted one of the suitcases.

Mitsi clutched Chubby Bear close. She sat.

"Want to see my new trick?" He wiggled a number two pencil between his thumb and forefinger. "It's called the Rubber Pencil."

There was only one magic trick Mitsi wanted Ted to perform and that was for him to wave his black wand and whisk them all home. She covered her ears to block out the sounds of the lady crying. *It cannot be helped*, Mitsi thought, remembering her grandmother's favorite expression. *It cannot be helped*. Even so, Mitsi wanted to sob, like their neighbor lady.

Instead, she said, "Yes. I want to see your new trick."

CHAPTER EIGHT

Freeze Tag

Mitsi had never eaten a Vienna sausage before, but in the first three days at Camp Harmony, they were served three times. That was three times too many. The first night, she'd reached under the table to slip her serving to Dash before she remembered he wasn't there. Another reason to miss him: *He* would have gobbled the disgusting things right up.

She also had never had to wait in such long lines to use a bathroom before. If you could call them bathrooms. They were more like the outhouse in Uncle Shig's field, only with more holes and more smells. And no dividers between the holes. No privacy. Mitsi tried holding it the second day; that was nearly a disaster. Then she found a cardboard box behind the canteen. It was big enough for her to sit under while she went. She could still hear other people, but she couldn't see them.

The food was awful, yet three times a day, at seven thirty and eleven thirty and five, Mitsi and her family waited outside the mess hall with everyone else in Area A, sometimes in the rain. At least it was something to do. There was a rumor of spaghetti for dinner tonight. Mitsi's favorite! She hoped it wasn't just a rumor.

Finally, they stepped into the dining room and picked up their trays. Mitsi sniffed the air. It sure smelled like spaghetti! When she saw someone twirling long strands of noodles around a fork, she almost cheered.

When it was her turn, she held up her tray. The server quickly dished up noodles and sauce and green beans, tucking a slice of bread on the side of the plate.

"There you go," he told Mitsi.

"Thank you." Mitsi scanned the room.

The news of a Vienna sausage–free meal had brought more people to the mess hall than usual. She stood on her tiptoes and looked all around to find five places together.

"I see some spots," Mom said. "This way." By the time they got there, two of them were taken.

"Over here. Over here." Three wrinkled ladies, looking like a trio of dried plums, waved to Obaachan. They slid together on the bench to make room. "Come. Sit."

Obaachan nodded. "For tonight," she said to Mom. She hobbled over to join the dried-plum ladies.

"Hey, Magic!" A boy jumped up, flagging Ted's attention.

"Hey, Frank. I mean, Lefty." Ted started to walk toward a table of junior high boys.

"Mom!" Mitsi couldn't believe it. He didn't even ask permission. "We have to sit together."

Mom sighed. "It's just for one night," she said.

Pop found a place for the three of them. He and Mom tucked into their dinners as if nothing was wrong. But Mitsi couldn't stomach one bite. She felt like she'd ridden too many times on the merry-go-round, dizzy and confused.

At home, each person had an assigned place. Pop sat at the head of the table, Mom at the foot near the stove so she could jump up quickly if she needed to get something. And she always seemed to need to jump up and get something. Ted sat on the wall side of the table, all by himself. Mitsi and Obaachan sat next to each other, opposite Ted, with Mitsi next to Pop and Obaachan next to Mom. No matter what was happening in the world, or at school, her heart always felt a little lighter after setting the table with five plates and five sets of silverware, each in their proper places. It was something to count on. Something she had always counted on.

Mitsi skipped dessert and went straight to their room after dinner. She opened up her suitcase, carefully folding her plaid dress and extra set of dungarees before placing them inside.

Ted ran in and grabbed his football. "What are you doing?"

"I want to be ready to go home," she told him. "As soon as General DeWitt says so."

"That might be a while," Ted said.

Mitsi ignored him and kept packing. There was something worse at this camp than eight-foot-high barbed wire fences and soldiers with guns at the gates. It was what was happening to her family. They were dandelion puffs being blown by the soft-est breeze.

"You're just going to have to unpack it tomorrow." Ted shook his head.

"Maybe not." Mitsi pushed a pair of stockings into the corner of the bag.

"Maybe so." Ted rolled the football in his hands, then ran outside.

Mitsi didn't care what he thought. She latched her bag when it was packed, and wedged it under her cot, right near her head, so she could grab it the second General DeWitt gave the word.

A few mornings later, the mess hall was nearly empty. A bad batch of Vienna sausages sent a lot of people to bed. Or running to the latrines. Since Mitsi's family had declared war on the vile things, they had dodged the diarrhea outbreak. Though they weren't in their proper places, the family sat together for three days straight. Mitsi actually began to relax, to feel like they could be a family again, even at this crummy camp.

But the bout of food poisoning passed, and one June morning, the mess hall was as crammed as ever. Ted grabbed his oatmeal and headed for the table with his new friends. They'd given one another nicknames: Ted was Magic, Henry was Tank, Tom was Skip, and Frank was Lefty. And Pudge was Pudge.

"Show us another trick, Magic," Tank said.

"Yeah, make my sister disappear," said Lefty. They all howled, like that was a real funny joke.

At the table with Mom and Pop — Obaachan was sitting with the dried-plum ladies — Mitsi stabbed her spoon at her bowl. Her mood was as lumpy as the oatmeal. It turned even lumpier when she stepped outside and right into a mud puddle.

"My anklet!" It looked like she'd dipped it into chocolate syrup. "It's ruined."

"Mud washes out," Mom said. "Thank goodness the laundry room is finally up and going. Let's go get you some clean socks." She reached for Mitsi's hand as though Mitsi was a little kid.

She shook her mother off. "I hate it here." She bent over and tried to wring the muddy water from the lace trim. It would never wash white again. "I want to go home."

Mom and Pop exchanged glances. Pop sighed. "I doubt you'll find one person who *wants* to be here."

Mitsi held up her hand like a traffic cop. "Don't say it. Don't say 'it cannot be helped.'"

"I wasn't going to." Pop nudged his hat farther back on his head. "I was going to say that we are lucky. Think of Mrs. Iseri and that young Mrs. Tokuda, whose husbands are far away. At least we are all together."

Mom slipped her arm around Pop's. "That's a big thing to be thankful for."

Mitsi didn't say anything. Lucky? They weren't lucky. And they weren't all together. What about Dash? And didn't Mom and Pop see what was happening with Ted? Even Obaachan had spent the past several afternoons drinking tea and knitting with the other grandmothers. Their family wasn't together. It was crumbling apart. Was she the only one who saw that?

"The time here won't seem so bad if you try to make the best of it," Mom continued. "What about asking those girls over there if you can play with them?" She pointed to three girls about Mitsi's age, crowded together on a stoop, out of the drizzle and mud, playing jacks.

"They look like they're having fun," Pop said.

"Jacks is a baby game. Besides, my sock is wet." Mitsi stomped off. At their room, she stripped off her socks and shoes and flopped onto her cot. The straw crinkled under her. Her leg began to itch. She scratched at two red bumps on her calf. It'd been a few days since the mattress had been aired out. It was probably full of fleas. How could you make the best of something so awful?

Mom and Pop stepped inside, shaking off their damp coats before hanging them on the hooks Pop had nailed to the wall. Mitsi rolled away from her parents, wrapping her arms around Chubby Bear. He smelled like Dash. It was too much. She tossed him to the foot of her bed. *Caddie Woodlawn* lay on the floor where she'd dropped it. Even though she'd practically memorized the book, she bent over and picked it up, flipping it open to a dog-eared page. Then she slapped it closed again. Her heart couldn't take the part about Caddie's dog dying. She rolled onto her back, covering her eyes with her arm.

"Why don't you get out your sketch pad and crayons?" Pop was piecing together some bits of scrap wood he'd collected. Like he was doing a jigsaw puzzle. "Or would you rather help me with Mom's nightstand?"

Mitsi peeked out from under her arm. The wood Pop was working with was all different colors, but the way he'd arranged them was beautiful. Prettier than anything Frederick & Nelson sold in their furniture department.

Mom rummaged around in her things. "Here you go." She held the art supplies out to Mitsi.

"I'm missing a long piece, here," Pop said. "I'll be back soon." He slipped back into his coat.

"I don't feel like drawing." Mitsi had gone to a lot of trouble to make that picture of Dash for the letter to General DeWitt, and what good had it done? It hadn't changed one thing. Mrs. Bowker was wrong after all. Mitsi couldn't make magic with her art. At least, not when it really mattered.

"Drawing might make the time pass more quickly." Mom set the pad and pencils on Mitsi's cot. "Wait, Shiro. I'll go with you." Her parents left together.

Nothing could make the time pass more quickly. Mitsi felt like she was in one long game of freeze tag. She had been tagged and nothing could unfreeze her. Not new friends, not anything. Except going home. To Dash. She felt herself turning to stone, like she really was frozen. She pulled a picture she'd drawn of Dash out of her sketch pad. It was the one of him with one ear up and one ear folded over; she stroked the page as if to unfold his ear. A tear plopped onto the drawing, wrinkling the top of Dash's muzzle. The more she looked at the picture, the worse she felt. It was too hard in this awful place without him. And too hard to think about him. Mitsi tore one long strip off the picture. Then another. Soon, there were a dozen long strips. She tore those into squares and then smaller squares. Before she knew what was happening, her drawing was a pile of confetti on her bed. Only confetti was for something good, like a party or a parade. She scooped up the mess and tossed it into the potbelly stove.

It would be breaking Mom's rules, but Mitsi had to get out of there. She tied her Keds and ran out the door. She kept running, past barrack after barrack. A stitch in her side slowed her up, but she kept running. She ran until she couldn't run anymore.

She found herself near the main gates. Dozens of people congregated outside the barbed wire fence. What were they doing? Every once in a while, Mitsi saw the flash of a camera: a reporter taking a photo for the newspaper. It'd probably be printed in the paper above a caption like JAPS HAPPY TO BE SAFE IN NEW HOMES, or some other kind of lie.

There were so many people near the gate that Mitsi wondered what would happen if she walked right through. Would one of the guards up there in that tower even be able to see her? Would there be an alarm? Would someone shoot?

Mitsi took a step toward the gate. And another.

Then someone grabbed her arm. She screamed.

"Geez Louise, Mits." Ted let go. "It's just me."

Mitsi swallowed her heart back into her chest. "What are you doing here?"

"Making money." Ted jingled coins in his pocket. "I racked up fifty cents yesterday."

Curiosity calmed her nerves. "How?"

"People from the outside come up and ask us to tell their friends that they've come to visit, and to meet them in the reception room." Ted tugged on his cap. "It doesn't even matter if you can't find them."

"You mean you take the money without delivering the message?"

"Well, I haven't. Not yet." Ted scratched a flea bite on his neck. "But Lefty has. He says someone like you could clean up because you look so sweet."

Mitsi stuck her tongue out at her brother.

"Of course, he doesn't know you very well." Ted grabbed Mitsi around the head and gave her a Dutch rub. "Besides, you're such a baby around strangers."

She wriggled loose from his grip. "I'm not a baby."

"Think of all those root beer barrels you could buy." Ted smacked his lips.

"I don't like root beer barrels," Mitsi lied.

"Suit yourself. Hey, Lefty!" Ted jogged away.

All that running had left Mitsi prickly and sweaty, but feeling miserable suited her fine right now. Why did Ted have to hang around with that Frank? And those stupid nicknames. Mitsi could think of a better one for Frank than Lefty: Goonbrain. She didn't like the way he was taking Ted over, like they were best buddies. There was something about Lefty that reminded her of a weasel. Or worse. She started back to her family's room, hoping she'd get back before Mom and Pop did. She wasn't supposed to go out in the camp by herself. Mitsi exhaled through her nose. She doubted they could think of any punishment worse than being in this rotten place.

On Tuesday, Mom read out loud from the Camp Harmony newsletter. "There's a movie tonight in the mess hall," she said. "Do you want to go?"

"No, thank you," said Mitsi.

On Wednesday, Obaachan said, "Come with me to knitting club."

"I want to finish my book," said Mitsi.

By Thursday, the rain had stopped and the sun began to dry up the mud and mess. Pop carried in another armful of scrap lumber. Now he was making Mom a small chest of drawers. "Some of the boys have made a couple of baseball teams and there's a game this afternoon. Shall we go watch?"

Everyone said yes, except Mitsi. "I'll get eaten alive by the mosquitos."

Mom and Pop shared a look over Mitsi's head. "It's not healthy to stay inside all the time," said Mom.

"I don't," said Mitsi. "I go to the mess hall. Three times a day." She turned the page and reread another chapter of *Caddie Woodlawn*.

On Friday, Mom held out Mitsi's shoes. "I've found out where Mrs. Tokuda lives. We're going to pay her a visit."

"I don't want to go." Mitsi pulled the scratchy olive-drab blanket over her head.

"I don't recall asking whether you wanted to or not." Mom dropped the shoes on the cot.

• • •

There were dark circles under Mrs. Tokuda's eyes that Mitsi hadn't remembered. "We'll watch the children." Mom picked up baby Donna. "You go take a nice long shower."

"I couldn't," said Mrs. Tokuda.

"Go." Mom rocked the baby in her arms. "You need the break."

While Mrs. Tokuda gathered her shower things, Mitsi gave Davy the set of blocks Pop had made from wood scraps. Over and over, he stacked them up and then, with a shriek of delight, knocked the tower down.

Mrs. Tokuda came back from the showers smelling of rosewater, toweling her damp hair. "That was heaven," she said. "Thank you so much."

Mitsi and Mom were a barracks or two away from their room when Mom stopped. "Oh, I left my hat!"

"I'll get it."

"We'll both go."

Mitsi put her hands on her hips. "Mom. I'm not a baby. It's not that far. I'll come right back."

"Wait until you're a mom, then you'll know how hard it is to let your little girl grow up." Mom tugged on Mitsi's braid. "Okay. Okay. Straight there and straight home."

"Mother!" Mitsi turned back toward Mrs. Tokuda's barracks.

The smell of cigarette smoke wafted around her head as she passed one of the shower houses. Pop didn't smoke, but lots of the men at camp did, especially the old guys. They'd get their last puffs in before heading in to shower. The shower room door was propped open and Mitsi caught a glimpse of a row of plaid bathrobes hanging from hooks outside the shower area.

And there was a person there, too. A kid. It looked like he was rifling through the pockets of one of the robes. Mitsi slowed. Looked again.

Lefty.

She backpedaled, searching for a place to get out of view. He came out, strutting down the steps. He didn't seem to see her. But she saw him. Stuffing something into the pockets of his chinos. Something that no doubt belonged to someone else.

Mitsi hung back until he was gone. Then she went to the Tokudas' and headed home, carrying a secret along with Mom's hat.

CHAPTER NINE

Love, Mitsi

"If it's Vienna sausages again, I'm not eating." Mitsi folded her arms across her chest.

"If it's Vienna sausages again," said Pop, "I'll join your hunger strike."

Mom clucked her tongue, but her father's joke made Mitsi smile, despite herself.

For the first time in ages, the Kashinos found five seats together in the mess hall. And at the same table as Mrs. Tokuda. Davy squirmed around, pretending to eat his chipped beef on toast. Little Donna slept in a baby seat on the bench.

"How are you doing?" Mom asked.

"Fine. Thank you." Mrs. Tokuda's hand went to a silver locket hanging around her neck.

"What a pretty necklace." Mom said the very words Mitsi was thinking.

Mrs. Tokuda opened the locket. "My husband. This way he is always near me." Like Mr. Iseri, Mr.

Tokuda had been sent to Fort Missoula. Mom, Obaachan, and Mitsi peered at the tiny photograph inside the locket. As tiny as it was, Mitsi could see that Mr. Tokuda looked like a very nice man. Like the kind of father who would give Davy horsey rides and sing "Rock-a-bye" to baby Donna.

Mitsi's hand went to her own neck, imagining just such a locket hanging there. With Dash's photo inside. Always near.

"I got a letter from him yesterday." Mrs. Tokuda clicked the locket shut. "That always makes things easier." The baby started to fuss.

"I could hold her while you eat," Mom offered.

"Oh, I couldn't." But Mrs. Tokuda looked like she could.

Mom reached for the baby.

Ted did a magic trick with the silverware, which made both Davy and Obaachan laugh. And Mitsi got Davy to eat almost all of his dinner by pretending each bite was an airplane zooming into the hangar.

The chipped beef wasn't as good as Mom's, but there was chocolate cake for after, and the man serving dessert gave Mitsi a piece with extra frosting.

Mrs. Tokuda skipped dessert. "Bedtime for these two," she explained.

"We'll look for you tomorrow," Mom said. After Mrs. Tokuda left, she turned to Mitsi. "You should go over there again. Entertain Davy so she can get a break."

"He likes Ted better." Mitsi dug into her cake. Ted didn't take the bait. She caught him glancing over his shoulder to the table where his friends were sitting. Friends! She glared at Lefty. She hadn't forgotten what she'd seen.

Ted pushed his plate aside. "May I be excused?" He scooted back on the bench, poised to jump up.

At home, no one left the table until everyone was finished. But now Pop said, "Sure, son."

Was she the only one who could see that Lefty meant trouble? All those good feelings drained away. The only dessert Mitsi wanted was family. All together. All in one place. And Ted away from Lefty. She picked at the rest of her cake.

A few minutes later, Ted returned with Lefty and some of his other new friends in tow. "We're going to see if there's any mail yet. You want to come along, Mits?"

"That's a good idea," said Mom.

Mitsi was about to say no, but Pop reached into his pocket and pulled out two quarters. "Get yourselves a treat at the canteen." He handed them the coins.

Mitsi had been to the canteen only once since it opened. With Mom, of course. Like the neighborhood store back home, it was stocked with Nehi sodas, penny candy, Popsicles, and bubble gum. Mitsi turned the coin over in her hand. No amount of money would buy what she really wanted.

"Come on, slowpoke!" Ted tugged Mitsi's sleeve.

"Go on." Mom waved her away. "Have some fun."

Fun. Right. With Ted and his dumb friends. She stayed put.

"Or you could come with Pop and me to the block meeting." Mom dabbed her mouth with her napkin.

Mitsi got up and followed Ted and his noisy crew. Why did they push each other around? All that shoving. It seemed so juvenile. She had never seen Ted act like this before. Maybe she should learn magic, too, so she could turn him back into the way he was before Camp Harmony.

The boys wound their way around this barrack and that, with Mitsi following a safe distance behind. They passed some younger boys gathered in a circle for a game of marbles. Frank — Lefty — stomped right through the circle, sending the marbles spinning away. He reached down and picked up an aggie, pocketing it with a swagger.

"Hey!" a kid yelled. "That's mine."

"Finders keepers." Lefty towered over the kid.

"Aw, let him have it back," Ted said.

Lefty gave Ted a look. Then he shrugged. "If you say so, Magic." He flicked the marble at the kid, clipping him on the shoulder. Mitsi noticed a marble at her feet. She picked it up and gave it to one of the younger boys.

"Is that your brother?" he asked, looking at Lefty.

"No." Mitsi pointed to Ted. "That one is."

The boy nodded. "Lucky for you," he said.

She nodded, too. Lucky for her. Ted was a nice guy. A good big brother. Why was he hanging around with a bully like Lefty? It didn't add up.

With a longing glance over her shoulder, Mitsi started after her brother and his so-called friends.

All those years of collecting for his paper route had made Ted brave with people he didn't know. He walked right into the little Area A post office and up to the man behind the window. "Kashino," he said. "The Shiro Kashino family."

The man flipped through a stack of letters. "Is Mitsi Kashino any relation?" he asked.

Mitsi's ears perked up. Ted pointed. "That's her."

"Well, it looks like you have some mail, little sister." The man smiled big around two missing teeth. Ted motioned her to come to the window, but Mitsi hung back near the door. Missing teeth were cute in first graders. Creepy in adults.

The man chuckled and passed an envelope through the grille in the window.

Ted glanced at the return address. "Guess who it's from." He brought the letter over to Mitsi, waving it above her head.

"Miss Wyatt?" she guessed, feeling guilty that she hadn't written to thank her teacher for the sketchbook.

Ted shook his head. She grabbed for the letter. "Mrs. Bowker?"

"Nope." He waggled the letter out of her reach.

"I can't guess." Mitsi crossed her arms. "Who is it from?"

Ted shrugged. "Heck if I know. Someone named D.K." He held it out to her.

"I've got it!" Lefty snagged the envelope and began to run.

"That's mine!" Mitsi chased him all the way to the canteen, where he stopped, holding the envelope over a garbage can. She ran at Lefty, but he stiff-armed her, smirking while she flailed away.

"That's enough." Ted jogged up to them. "Give it to her."

"*Give* it to her? Make me." Lefty jabbed the envelope at Mitsi with one hand, and boxed at Ted with the other. Ted boxed back and they roughhoused around. What a bunch of baboons. While Lefty was deflecting one of Ted's swings, she snatched the envelope away, smoothing it out.

"Come on, guys." Pudge jerked his thumb toward the canteen. "I want to get a Baby Ruth." That broke up the wrestling match, but the boys kept clowning around when they got inside the store. Mitsi stayed far away from them; she could see trouble coming. And it did. Someone shoved Lefty, and when he shoved back, a tower of saltine cracker boxes cascaded to the floor.

The canteen manager hustled out from behind the counter. "You boys want to come back here again, you pick that up." He pointed at the mess. "Pronto."

The boys stopped laughing. Even though he hadn't knocked them over, Ted started picking up boxes right away. So did Pudge. Finally, Lefty helped, too.

Disgusted with the boys, Mitsi turned her attention to the envelope in her hands. It was postmarked Seattle. But who was D.K.?

She peeled back the flap and pulled out a typewritten letter.

Dear Mitsi,

I am doing fine. That bone you left for me is safely buried under Mrs. Bowker's dahlias. Today, I chased three squirrels but didn't catch any. I'm sure I'll catch one tomorrow!

I had a hard time the first night here. Mrs. Bowker petted me until I fell asleep. It wasn't the same as sleeping with you, but it helped.

We walked over to the drugstore to take in some film to be developed. Mrs. Bowker says soon she will have something extra special to mail to you. I don't think it will be a bone. That wouldn't fit in a letter.

Mrs. Bowker says to tell you I am a very good dog. I haven't chewed one slipper or chased one car.

Woof! Woof!

Dash

The boys argued over how Ted should spend his quarter. Mitsi tuned them out. She also tuned out the chime of the cash register and the door creaking open and closed. All she could think about was Dash. She read the letter three times.

"Ready to head back, Mits?" Ted asked.

"What?" She shook her head, as if waking up from a long nap. Ted was munching on a long rope of something red. She shook her head again, coming back to earth. There was her brother chewing on a red licorice rope. She blinked. What was on that display behind him? Paper. Pens.

"In a minute." She picked out and paid for some writing materials. Mom already had stamps.

Mitsi carried her purchases and the letter from Dash back to their room.

"I knew Dash could speak and roll over," Pop teased, "but I didn't know he could write."

Mitsi made a little desk by balancing her suitcase on her knees. She thought hard about what she would write before she put one stroke of the pen to paper. She didn't want to send a letter with any cross-outs. She knew it wasn't Dash writing to her. Mrs. Bowker was just being nice. But it was fun thinking of writing to him. Fun to think of writing to her one true friend. And she didn't know anyone else with a four-legged pen pal. She picked up the pen and began.

Dear Dash,

It sounds like you're having a good time at Mrs. Bowker's house. I know you're an expert digger, but please don't dig up anything. Especially not the tulips.

Maybe it is a good thing you couldn't come here. We're squeezed together in one room like sardines in a can. I have to crawl across Ted's cot to go to bed.

We get a lot of Vienna sausages. If you were here, I would be happy to share.

Mitsi sat back. It might make Dash and Mrs. Bowker sad if she told them too much about Camp Harmony. But they were her best friends. They'd want to know the truth. Mitsi started writing again.

There are a lot of things I don't like here. I don't like waiting in line to use the bathroom. I don't like everyone sitting in the wrong places at dinner. And I don't like hearing the people on the other side of the wall. The man snores and the lady cries.

But there is one thing I do like. Hearing from you. Please keep writing.

Love,

Mitsi

CHAPTER TEN

Muddy Buddies

Mom wouldn't let Mitsi go to the post office by herself. "Ted can walk you," she said.

"But I know the way," Mitsi argued.

"Did I say you didn't?" Mom took another stitch on the patch for Ted's dungarees.

Mitsi blew her bangs off her forehead. She would never win this argument. Mom still thought of her as a baby, even though she'd be twelve in a few weeks.

"What's it worth to you?" Ted asked Mitsi.

Mom glowered. "Your brother would be delighted to escort you." She tied a knot in the thread, then snipped it off.

Ted grabbed his baseball cap. "Come on if you're coming."

It took forever to get there. First, some little kids came running up and asked Ted to show them the Rubber Pencil trick. Of course, he did. Then they walked past the barracks where those boys had been playing marbles. They were getting set up again and closed ranks when they saw Ted.

"What do you want?" asked the aggie boy.

"Sorry about yesterday." Ted reached into his pocket and pulled out a handful of marbles. "I'm not going to use these anymore. You guys can have them."

"Hey, swell!" A skinny kid with holes in the knees of his corduroys jumped up. He cradled the marbles in his fist, counting. "Three for each of us!" He divvied them out to his friends.

The aggie boy rolled his share in his hand. "You could play if you want."

"I have to take my kid sister to the post office." Ted jerked his thumb toward Mitsi.

The skinny kid laughed. "Gonna mail her somewhere?" The other boys joined in.

Ted stroked a pretend beard, as if considering the idea. "Aw, I guess not. She's a pretty good egg."

Mitsi stuck her tongue out at him and stomped off. Why did Ted have to tease her like that?

"Wrong way!" Ted called out. The marbles boys laughed.

Mitsi turned around. "I did that on purpose." She hoped at least one kid would believe her.

Several barracks over, Obaachan's friend, Mr. Hirai, stopped them to ask if their grandmother was over her cold. Mitsi hung back, behind Ted.

Mr. Hirai was old. His teeth clicked when he talked. Sometimes the top ones slid all the way out of his mouth. It never bothered him. He'd just push them back in. But it gave Mitsi the willies.

"She said to thank you for that special tea," Ted said.

"That is good for colds, that tea." Mr. Hirai leaned on his walking stick. "I drink that every day of my life. Never get sick. Not even gas!" He tapped his stick for emphasis. Ted busted up, but Mitsi felt the heat rise from her neck to her cheeks, like the mercury in a thermometer. Old people didn't care what they said sometimes.

Finally, Mr. Hirai took a breath and Ted jumped in. "We better get going," he said. "Mom will expect us back."

"Fine, yes." Mr. Hirai waved his free hand. "Obey thy mother and father." He reached toward Mitsi to pat her head. "You are good children. Not like some here." He clucked his tongue. "Taking money from old men."

Mitsi shot a quick glance at Ted, thinking about Lefty. There'd been notices posted in the shower houses about not leaving valuables in pants and robe pockets. One of their neighbors had lost ten whole dollars before volunteers started keeping a closer eye on things.

"That is crummy." Ted shook his head. "We've got to get going," he said. "Sayonara."

After all that waiting to get to the post office, Mitsi lost her nerve when she stepped inside. The man with the missing teeth was behind the counter again. She tugged on Ted's arm. "Will you mail it for me?" She held out the letter.

"Grow up." Ted pushed her away. "Mom's never going to let you go places by yourself if you don't cut the shy act."

"Just this once?" Mitsi made puppy-dog eyes. "Please?"

Ted let out a big sigh. He took the letter and slid it through the bars in the window. "We'd like to mail this."

"Sure enough." The man tossed the envelope behind him into a big bin. He noticed Mitsi by the door. "Kashino, right?"

Mitsi looked at Ted, barely nodding.

"Kashino," Ted repeated. He stood up extra tall. "A-52-101," he said, giving their full Camp Harmony address.

The man rubbed his chin. "I think I got something for you." He disappeared for a moment. When he came back, Mitsi could see he was holding two letters! He passed them through the grille to Ted. Mitsi ran over to see who'd sent them.

"Are they both for me?" She danced around Ted like Dash used to dance around her when she held out a treat.

"Don't be a greedy-guts. This one's to Mom and Pop." Ted put one letter in his shirt pocket. He tapped the other against his hand. "What's this worth to you?"

"No fair!" She put her hands on her hips. "Give it here."

"Maybe your dessert for the next two nights?"

She squinted. "One night."

He scratched his head with the envelope, thinking it over. "Okay. Deal." He tossed it to her.

She ripped it open, unfolding the letter right there in the post office.

"Looks like you lost something there." The post office man pointed at the floor.

Ted handed it to her.

"Oh, it's the picture Mrs. Bowker took of Dash and me!" Mitsi ran her fingers over it. He seemed so close, she could almost feel his soft fur.

"Who's Dash?" Post Office Man leaned over the counter.

Mitsi was so excited, she forgot all about being afraid of him and his missing-teeth smile. She walked over to the window. "My dog." She held up the photo.

The man smiled. Mitsi could see that his blue eyes had a twinkle in them. "That is one good-looking pup," he said. "I bet he's smart as a whip."

"He can sit, shake, and say his prayers." Her heart clenched up as she studied the photo. She was glad to have it, but it made her miss Dash all the more. "And he's a magician. He makes cookies disappear!"

The post office man laughed.

Mitsi talked Ted into walking home by way of the Tokudas' barracks. When Davy saw the picture of Dash, he clapped his pudgy hands. "Doggy say ruff-ruff." Mrs. Tokuda jiggled the baby in her arms, smiling. "That's right, honey. Ruff-ruff." Her locket bounced against her neck as she swung the baby back and forth.

Mr. Hirai was sitting on a box outside his room. "Ah," he said. "I had a dog like that once, too. Fido." He told a long story about Fido. Even though his top teeth slipped out twice, Mitsi listened with interest.

"You really taught him to count to three?" Mitsi wondered if Dash could learn that, too.

"Like this." Mr. Hirai tipped his head back and barked three times. He sounded like a real dog. "See? Three." He looked at Mitsi and began to chuckle. She couldn't help joining in.

"See you later, Mr. Hirai." Mitsi and Ted started off again, but they hadn't gone far when they met the dried-plum ladies sitting in a row, knitting. They wanted to see the photo, too. "Oooh," said the plum ladies, their needles clicking in time.

"Look at those bright eyes," said one.

"And those floppy ears," said another.

"Better-looking than Fala," said the third. Mitsi had to agree. The president's dog wasn't near as handsome as Dash.

"Come on, Mits." Ted tugged on her sleeve. "I was supposed to meet the guys twenty minutes ago."

Mitsi hurried along. But she couldn't help it if people she didn't even know asked to see Dash's photo. She wondered how they'd heard about it!

She saved the letter until she got home. Finally, she sat on her cot, ready to read.

Dear Mitsi,

Mrs. Bowker's peonies are blooming now. They are especially beautiful because of the bone I buried under the biggest bush.

We went for a drive yesterday. Mrs. Bowker took me to a place called a bank. I felt sorry for her because she only got some funny green paper to put in her pocketbook, while I got a dog biscuit from the bank manager himself! Yum! Afterward, we stopped at the butcher for more bones. And then we went to visit Mrs. Bowker's cousin, who has a nice dog named Bandit. Bandit and I played "Chase around the Maple Tree," and "See Who Can Bark the Loudest," and also "Tug-of-War." After that, Mrs. Bowker and I went home. Then I took a long, long nap. Mrs. Bowker said I was so tired, I snored.

I go for a walk every day, right by our old house; I make a wish on the lamppost. I bet you know what I'm wishing for. We check the lock and look around to make sure everything is okay. It is.

I hear the bag of dog food rattling. That means suppertime!

I'll write again tomorrow.

Your pal,

Dash

It sounded like Dash was having a good time with Mrs. Bowker.

But, hopefully, not too good a time. Mitsi set the photo on her pillow. Though she couldn't see it in the picture, she knew Dash's tail was wagging because of that big doggy smile. And that doggy smile made her smile, too, even though she missed him like crazy. That was funny about the lamppost; she didn't remember telling Mrs. Bowker about how she and Mags used to make wishes on it. Mitsi made another wish now, for a locket like Mrs. Tokuda's, so she could carry Dash with her wherever she went. At least until they could be together again.

She picked up her pen to write back.

Dear Dash,

I'm glad you made a new buddy. Bandit sounds nice. I made some new friends, too, when I showed off your picture. Everyone thinks you're handsome. Mr. Hirai used to have a dog like you, too, and said he taught him to count to three. He might have been pulling my leg. But I bet you could learn to count to five.

Tonight they're showing a Mickey Mouse movie after supper and I'm going to watch it with Mom and Pop. I know how much you like Mickey Mouse. Wish you were here to watch it with me.

Be a good boy!

Love,

Mitsi

• • •

Every day, Mitsi went to the post office to check for a letter from Dash. Ted went with her but would ditch her if he saw Lefty and the rest of their gang. Mitsi finally convinced Mom that the walk to the post office wasn't any farther than going to her old school. With a lot more neighbors watching out for her along the way.

She was headed home with another letter when she noticed an older teenager sitting on a fruit crate, balancing a sketchbook on his knees. His hand darted like a bird over the paper. Mitsi stopped, watching from a distance.

"I don't bite," the kid said, not even looking up from the sketch pad. "You want to see what I'm doing?"

Mitsi edged closer. "It's just one of the barracks," she said when she saw the image on the page. A barracks with the door and window wide open against the heat. Why would anyone want to draw a dumpy old building?

"I'd rather be drawing something else. But this is what's here, right?"

That made sense. Mitsi stood quietly while the guy finished the picture. In the bottom left-hand corner, he wrote his name. Eddie Sato. Next to his signature, he drew an ant.

She pointed at the ant. "What's that for?"

"Ants are hard workers, right?" He shrugged. "Artists gotta be hard workers, too. Always drawing. Always looking."

If she were going to draw something next to her

signature, it wouldn't be an ant. It'd be something cuter. Like a dog. Still, Mitsi watched as Eddie wrote something else at the bottom of the page.

"'Air conditioning,'" Mitsi read aloud. She grinned. "That's pretty funny." It was like that joke Pop used to make about their car having air conditioning — as long as they rolled all the windows down.

Eddie flipped to a fresh page. "Just because they put us here, doesn't mean we have to roll over and take it. Right?" He handed the sketch pad to her. "You want to try something?"

"No." Mitsi shook her head. "No, thanks. I've got to get going." It had already taken her twice as long to get home because of all the people who'd stopped to ask her what was new with Dash. Mom would worry. "Maybe another time."

"See you around." Eddie shifted on his crate, turning to face a different direction, and started drawing again. With only a few strokes on the page, Mitsi could see that he was drawing the guard tower that loomed over the camp.

"See you." Mitsi wondered what kind of caption Eddie would put on that new picture. What kind of caption would she write if it were her drawing? It wouldn't be anything funny, like Eddie's, that was for sure.

"Mitsi, Mitsi!" The cook whose nose looked like a cauliflower came running out of the mess hall. "I made something for you." He handed her a Popsicle-stick picture frame.

Mitsi pulled her treasured photo from her shorts pocket. "It's a perfect fit. Thank you." Dash's face popped right out at her.

"It's nothing. Now, be sure to tell Mrs. Bowker that milk's not good for dogs."

"I will." Mitsi nodded. No one made fun of her for getting mail from a dog. Everyone seemed to like the idea. Even the grown-ups.

Cauliflower Cook smoothed his white apron across his watermelon belly. "I wish they'd let him come, at least for a visit. That'd perk up this place in no time." He patted Mitsi's shoulder and went back inside to his work.

Mitsi started to tuck Dash's photo back in her pocket when she noticed a girl, about her age, perched on a nearby stoop. She was bent over a book, nose nearly to the page. Mitsi wasn't sure what came over her, but she called out to the girl. "What are you reading?"

The girl marked her place with her finger, looking up. Squinting. *Thimble Summer.* What's that picture of?"

Mitsi held out the snapshot. "My dog. Dash."

The girl hopped up from the stoop. "I bet it's the best, having a dog. May I?"

Mitsi nodded, and the girl took the photo, holding it closer to her face. "My glasses got broken. Mom sent money to a friend outside to buy me a new pair." She handed the photo back. "He looks like a sweetheart."

"He is. You want to know my favorite thing?" When Mitsi talked about Dash with strangers, she didn't feel so shy. "Sometimes, he would sleep with his head right here." She pointed to the side of her neck. "When he did that, I felt like nothing could ever go wrong. That as long as he was with me, I'd be safe." She rested her hand on her neck, remembering. "Hey, are you okay?"

A tear trickled down the girl's cheek. She brushed it away and plunked back down on the stoop. "I couldn't have a dog because they make my dad sneeze. His eyes swell up like this." She bugged her eyes out to demonstrate.

"Maybe you could have one when you're older."

The girl rested her chin on her hands. "I'd rather have my dad."

Mitsi didn't know what to say. The girl seemed lonely. Sad. Like she didn't have a friend.

Mitsi tucked the snapshot back in her pocket. "Do you want to go for a walk?"

The girl jumped up. "I gotta ask my mom." She stopped, her hand on the door handle. "What's your name?" Mitsi told her. "I'm Debbie. Be right back." She ran inside her room and was back in a heartbeat. "Mom said yes!" Debbie waved an envelope. "Can we go to the post office to mail this for Mom?"

Mitsi smiled. What would Mel say? Twice in one day. "Sure," she answered.

Debbie jumped off the stoop, sailing over all three steps.

"What shall we do?" Debbie brushed herself off when she landed.

Mitsi wrinkled her forehead. "I thought we were going to the post office."

Debbie flapped her hand dismissively. "*While* we're walking," she clarified.

"We don't just walk?"

"Never! Too boring." Debbie snapped her fingers. "I've got it. We have to do two pliés for every old lady we see."

"How old?" Mitsi asked. "And what's a plié?"

"Old." She bent her legs to the side so that they looked like pointed parentheses. "I study ballet." She rose back to standing, her arms graceful as swans. "Well, I did." She shrugged. "I used to do lots of things."

Mitsi nodded. She used to do lots of things, too. Like being the filling in a Mitsi sandwich with Judy and Mags. Or playing jacks at recess. Even going to school. It was a nice feeling to walk along with someone who knew about giving up things that mattered.

"Plié!" Debbie bent down and up twice.

"That lady wasn't old," Mitsi said. "She looks like my mom's age."

"Well, that's older than us, right?"

Mitsi couldn't argue with that. She pliéd, though not as gracefully as Debbie. "Hey, did you say your mom was getting you glasses from outside?"

Debbie twirled on her tippy-toes. "They should be here any day."

"How did she do it?"

Debbie twirled again and again and again. "Wow. Everything's spinning." She braced herself on the corner of the nearest barracks. "Woo." She pressed her fingers against her temples. "I forgot to spot."

Mitsi had never met anyone quite as enthusiastic as Debbie. It was no wonder she was green-bean thin, with all that jumping and twirling and pliéing.

"She just wrote a letter," Debbie said.

"What?" Now Mitsi felt like she was the one who'd been twirling around.

"Mom. She wrote to one of our friends, sent them the money, and they bought my glasses." Debbie drew her fingers to a point on either side of her eyes. "Cat's-eye frames. Blue."

"Those will look good on you." Mitsi did a little twirl herself. What if she wrote to Mrs. Bowker and asked her to buy a locket for Dash's photo? She rested her fingers on her throat. With a locket, she could carry *him* with her everywhere.

One small problem. How would she pay for it?

"Favorite book?" Debbie quizzed.

"What? Oh, Betsy, Tacy —" Mitsi stopped. The Betsy, Tacy, and Tib books *had* been her favorites. Back when things like Mitsi sandwiches still existed. "*Caddie Woodlawn*," she said.

Debbie did a cheerleader jump. "Mine, too!"

"I brought a copy," Mitsi offered. "If you didn't."

"Oh, my gosh!" Debbie hopped in circles around Mitsi. "And you can borrow anything from me. I have a regular library. I even brought a set of encyclopedias." She clapped her hands to either side of her cheeks. "I can't believe it. You brought *Caddie Woodlawn*!"

As they neared the Area A post office by the main gate, Mitsi could see crowds of people on the other side of the high fence. She remembered what Ted had said about delivering messages. And how Lefty said she'd be good at it.

But it would mean talking to strangers. A lot of strangers. Mitsi wasn't sure she could do that. Not even for a locket.

"Aren't you coming?" Debbie held the door open, kicking dirt off her shoes.

"Oh, yeah. Sorry." Mitsi stamped her feet, too,

then followed Debbie inside, walking the letter over to the man with the missing teeth. "Hi, Mel."

"Well, hey, Mitsi. Long time, no see." He chuckled because he saw her nearly every day. "Who's your partner in crime there?"

"This is Debbie." Mitsi tugged her forward. "We're in the same grade." She stood on tiptoes to hand the envelope to Mel. "Anything today?"

He shook his head. "Sorry about that."

"Maybe tomorrow," Mitsi said.

"That's the attitude." Mel saluted her. "Nice to meet you, Debbie."

Debbie nodded. The girls went back outside.

"You are so brave!" Debbie shivered. "He's kind of creepy-looking."

"I was a little scared of him at first, too." The truth was that she'd been a lot afraid of Mel. "But not anymore." Two old ladies passed them, walking arm in arm. Mitsi bent her knees.

"No more pliés." Debbie held up her hand. "I challenge you to a game of hink pink. I'll go first." She scrunched up her face, thinking. "Got it! A hog's hairpiece."

Mitsi took a wild guess. "Pig wig!"

Debbie grinned. "Your turn."

"A rodent's residence."

Debbie whooped. "Mouse house!" They played back and forth, moving on to Hinky Pinky, where Mitsi stumped her with "a baseball player who just got a raise."

"I have no idea." Debbie shook her head. "I don't know much about baseball."

Mitsi giggled. "A richer pitcher!"

"I'm going to remember that one!" They'd reached Debbie's barracks. She hopped up each step, pausing at the top with her hand on the doorknob. "This was my best day in camp."

"Mine, too." Mitsi paused. "Maybe I'll see you tomorrow?"

"I'll be your friend who fell in the dirt." Debbie held up her dirty shoes. Even when it wasn't raining, it was impossible to stay out of the muck. "Your muddy buddy, get it?"

"Got it! See you tomorrow?"

"It's a date!" Debbie disappeared inside her room.

Mitsi smiled. Wasn't it funny that someone like Debbie thought *Mitsi* was brave? All because she talked to Mel. Maybe she *could* be brave enough to talk to strangers. Mitsi took careful steps to dodge another mud puddle. She wondered how much a locket like Mrs. Tokuda's cost.

The little runny-nosed boy from Block 3 ran up behind Mitsi, tugging on her shirt. "I'm gonna get a dog just like yours when I grow up."

"I bet you will," Mitsi told him. She crossed the way toward Barracks 52. Somehow the mud didn't seem so muddy. The buildings seemed more solid. Mitsi thought she could even see a bit of blue sky behind the clouds above.

"A penny for your thoughts," Pop said that night at dinner. Mitsi was cozied between him and Mom.

Mitsi took a sip of her milk. "I was thinking that Dash really is a magician, like Ted."

"He is?" Pop said.

"Yep." Obaachan and the dried-plum ladies waved at her from their table. Mitsi waved back. "Even from far away, he's turning this camp into a friendlier place."

Pop wrapped his arm around her shoulders and squeezed her close. Mitsi poked at her burned scalloped potatoes. "I just wish he could do something about the food!"

CHAPTER ELEVEN

Three Dollars and Ninety-Five Cents

Mitsi gobbled up her oatmeal and downed her milk. "May I be excused?"

"Where's the fire?" Pop asked.

"Are you going to go play with that girl you met yesterday?" Mom asked. "Debbie?"

"Yeah. And I'm kind of late." It was true that Mitsi was going to play with Debbie. Just not today; Debbie had gotten a pass out of camp with her mom for some reason. She said they'd be gone for a few days. And it was true that Mitsi was late. What if other kids beat her to the fence, got all the jobs? Mitsi slid off the bench. "See you at lunch."

It had rained again overnight and the mud puddles were mucky booby traps. She tried to weave around them, but there were too many. Her shoes looked two sizes bigger by the time she got to the fence. She scraped the mud off as best she could on one of the posts. She wanted to make a good impression.

There were tons of kids like Mitsi hanging around. But there were lots of people outside the fence, too. There could be jobs for all of them. Ted and Lefty and those other boys were bunched up not far from the sentry post. She staked out a spot as far away from them as she could.

Imagining the cool weight of a locket on her neck, Mitsi took a deep breath for courage, then edged closer to the fence. It wasn't long before she heard, "Little girl. Little girl," and spied a woman waving at her. Mitsi angled closer to where the woman was standing, the fence a tall, prickly wall between them. "Do you know the Terados?" the woman asked.

"I know Mrs. Tokuda," she offered.

"Terado." The woman fished a piece of paper from her pocketbook. "Area A, Barracks 30, Apartment 4."

Thirty wasn't too far from the gate. "I can run tell them you're here," Mitsi said.

"Oh, thank you. Thank you."

Mitsi stood there, wondering when the money part happened.

"Apartment 4, you said?"

"Yes. A-30-4." The woman opened her pocketbook but only to put away the piece of paper.

"Okay. Who shall I say is here?" Mitsi put her hands in her pockets, fluffing them out, hoping the woman would get the idea.

"Mae Lindquist," she said. "Their neighbor."

"Lindquist." Mitsi nodded. "Okay."

"I'll meet them in there." Mae Lindquist pointed at the reception room.

Mitsi sighed. "I'll tell them." So much for easy money!

She delivered the message and ran back to the fence. Some other kids were in her spot now. One kid pocketed a whole quarter for taking a message.

"Hello. Hello!" A teenager flagged Mitsi's attention. "I'm looking for Ellen Hayashi. Do you know her?"

"Do you have her address?" Mitsi asked.

The girl gave it to her. It was close by, too. "Be right back!" Mitsi started off.

"Wait, wait!" The teenager stuck her hand through the fence. "Here's something for your trouble."

Mitsi took the dime. "Thank you!" After delivering that message, Mitsi got three more to deliver and three more tips. As the morning went on, she moved slower and slower, weighed down by the goo caking up on her shoes. By lunchtime, forty-five cents jingled in her pocket.

And her shoes were bricks of mud. Too mucky to wear inside, she left them outside the mess hall. She got her tray, found Mom and Pop sitting with Mrs. Iseri. Mom didn't comment on Mitsi's stocking feet. She and Mrs. Iseri were studying a Sears, Roebuck catalog.

"I can't take the fleas anymore. I'm sending for that mattress," Mrs. Iseri said. "Reverend Andrews said he could bring it down in his truck." She sneezed. "And I think I'm allergic to hay!"

"You poor thing." Mom patted her arm. "Do you mind if I look through the catalog later? Ted needs new trousers. He's grown an inch since we arrived. At least."

Mrs. Iseri pushed the catalog toward her. "I'm done with it for now." She poked at the cabbage roll on her plate. "I think I'm done with this, too." She made a face and shoved her plate aside. "Could I get you some more tea?"

"I'd love some." Mom stood up, too. "But I'll come with you."

Mitsi turned the catalog around and began flipping through it. There had to be a section with lockets. She licked her finger, turning page after page, faster and faster. Finally, after washing machines and lingerie and baby clothes, she found the jewelry. She pored over the page. There at the bottom was a picture of a locket like the one she'd imagined. A silver oval, with a curlicue design on the front, hanging from a silver chain. She read the description, then ran her finger over to the price. Three dollars and ninety-five cents. It had taken her three hours to earn forty-five cents. At this rate, she'd have to work twenty-seven hours.

She shut the catalog and did some mental math. If she worked three hours every day, it would take . . . nine days. She let her head drop to the table. Nine days!

"Are you feeling okay?" Mom placed her hand on the back of Mitsi's head. Mitsi sat up.

"Yes." She sighed. "Mom, do you have any chores I could do?"

"Now I know you're not feeling well." Mom laughed. "What kind of chores?"

"Chores that I could get paid for?"

Mom shook her head. "Mitsi, you know how Pop and I feel about that. We're all part of this family —"

"So we all do our part." Mitsi picked a raisin out of the carrot-raisin salad on her plate and put it in her mouth. She didn't even like raisins.

"I could use a hand," Mrs. Iseri said. "Carrying my laundry basket to the laundry house."

Mitsi perked up. "Okay!" This was more like it.

Mom gave Mitsi the look.

"I mean, I'd be happy to do that, Mrs. Iseri." Mitsi swallowed the raisin. "No charge."

"Thank you, dear." Mrs. Iseri reached across the table to tap Mitsi's hand. "Are you free tomorrow after breakfast?"

Mitsi couldn't believe it. She had gotten herself into a pickle. "Sure."

After lunch, Mitsi picked up her shoes from outside the mess hall. She sat on the fence rail to put them on. Clumps of mud dangled from the laces like dried-up slugs.

"That's a big mess," Mr. Hirai observed as he passed by.

"I know," Mitsi said. "I'm a mud magnet." She finished tying her sneakers and clomped off. "See you later!"

Rain pounding on the roof woke Mitsi later that night. Thunder rumbled in the distance and, *pow*, a bolt of lightning lit up the room. Mitsi blinked to clear her vision. It seemed like the door was moving, one tiny inch at a time. She blinked again and caught Ted sliding through the opening and into the room. He shrugged out of his jacket and jeans, sending a wave of something stale in Mitsi's direction. Cigarette smoke. She scrunched her eyes closed so he wouldn't know she was awake. When had he gone out? And where? It didn't take a genius to figure out that this mystery had something to do with Lefty.

The cot next to her creaked as Ted got under the covers. He was snoring in no time. She leaned up on one elbow. Asleep, he looked as innocent as a baby. She lay back down, saying a prayer that he was.

Overnight, the storm turned the camp walkways to chocolate sludge. Right after breakfast, Mitsi slogged her way to the front gate. She got a job first thing. But it was a message for some people at the very far end of Area A, in Barracks 96.

It would take her forever to get there. And they'd only given her a ten-cent tip. She reached for the dime in her pocket. They wouldn't know if she didn't deliver the message. Lots of kids took tips and didn't follow through. She tugged her foot out of a pile of goo. Not lots of kids. One kid. Lefty. She started off again. This time, the goo grabbed her shoe and didn't let go. She walked right out of it.

"Augh!" She screamed at the top of her lungs. "Stupid mud." Stupid camp. Stupid everything.

"You okay?" Mr. Hirai hobbled toward her.

"Yes. No. Look at me." She tugged to free her shoe. "I was just trying to —" Frustration choked off the rest of the sentence.

"I see." He rubbed his chin. "Looks like you could use some help."

"I could use some money," she said.

He threw his head back and laughed. "Money is rarely the answer," he said. He waved her closer. "Come. Come with me."

"I have to —"

"Come." Mr. Hirai started back toward his room.

Mitsi followed, hopping on one foot. She waited on the stoop while he went inside.

"Here is your answer." He presented her with a pair of wooden sandals.

"Getas?" They were so old-fashioned! Only the elderly Japanese people wore them anymore. "Very nice," she said politely.

He chuckled, turning the getas sideways so Mitsi could see the long "teeth" on the bottom. "These are perfect for walking in this mud." He placed them in her hands. "It seems very important for you to be walking in this mud." Then he tilted his head back and barked three times. "Maybe something to do with Dash?"

Mitsi looked at him. How on earth did he know? "Thank you." She sat down on the stoop, pulled off her one shoe and her socks, and slipped the *hanao*, the cloth thong, between her big toes. It felt a little funny. She stood up. The teeth of the sandals clip-clopped against the wooden stoop.

Mr. Hirai chuckled. "Music to my ears."

Mitsi carefully placed her foot down on the top step and then the next. Her ankles wobbled, but she thought she was getting the hang of it. When she reached the last step, she toppled off the getas.

"Takes some practice," Mr. Hirai said.

Mitsi took a few steps away from the stoop to the path where the dirt was soft and mucky. She plunked her foot down. "Hey, look!" The teeth of the sandal sunk down, yet her foot was safe from the mud. "These are great."

"You aren't the only one who thinks so." He spread his arms far apart. "There's a list of people this long that want them. And the younger men don't know how to make them. Only old coots like me."

Mitsi teetered over to Mr. Hirai and threw her arms around his neck. "You aren't an old coot," she said, a bit embarrassed that she used to think so herself. "Thank you." She picked up her shoes and socks and made her way back to the front gate, where she got five more jobs and two more tips.

Then she clomped home. Done for the night.

"I'm back!" Debbie called from her front stoop.

"Good-looking glasses."

Debbie posed. "Do you like them?"

Mitsi nodded.

Debbie noticed Mitsi's feet. "I used to have some of those." She looked down at her own muddy shoes. "I bet they come in handy here."

"Mr. Hirai's making some, if you want a pair. And they do come in handy." Mitsi smiled. Thanks to the getas, it'd been no trouble getting around that afternoon. She'd earned another dollar. Only two dollars and fifty cents to go. "Do you want to go to the movie tonight? I think it's *Pinocchio*."

Debbie pretended her arms were on strings, like a puppet's. "I'll meet you after supper."

"See you later, then," said Mitsi.

Debbie pointed to her glasses. "I will definitely see you later."

CHAPTER TWELVE

Camp Birthday

Mitsi was awakened by the "Happy Birthday" song.

"You look like a monkey" — Ted's voice wobbled like an opera singer's — "and you smell like one, too!"

She threw her pillow at him, catching him on the ear.

"I'm hit!" Ted crashed to the floor, flopping around like a dying fish. "Good-bye, cruel world."

"Settle down." Mom unrolled her pin curls. "You'll wake the neighbors."

Even Pop had to laugh at that. "A sneezing spider would wake the neighbors," he pointed out.

Mom fluffed her hair. "He still needs to settle down."

Mitsi clambered over Ted's cot and stretched.

"Twelve years old." Mom gave her a kiss. "How did that happen?"

"This isn't much." Pop held out a small bundle, tied up in a red bandanna. Mitsi undid the knots.

"A treasure box!" Pop had become a wizard at making things out of the scraps of wood left over from building Camp Harmony. She knew she shouldn't hope for anything more, but maybe there'd be some birthday money inside. All she needed was fifty more cents to send for the locket. She lifted the lid. Empty. Still, she breathed in the smell of new wood. "It's beautiful."

"Mom painted the flowers on top," Pop said. "And Obaachan figured out how to line it with flannel."

"One of my old shirts," Ted said. "So I helped, too."

Mitsi cradled the box to her chest. Her family had worked hard to give her this one gift. "I know what I'll keep in here." She gathered Dash's letters from under the cot and set them inside. "Thank you." She hugged everyone, even Ted.

Back home, a birthday breakfast was special, even if it fell on a school morning. Mom's job was to mix up buttermilk waffles and Pop's was to measure the birthday kid. A railroad track of pencil marks crosshatched the kitchen door frame: *Teddy, age 3, 33 inches; Mitsi, age 5, 40 inches.* Last year, on her eleventh birthday, she'd been as tall as Ted had been on *his* eleventh birthday: fifty-two inches. She'd grown a little this past year, but she doubted she'd ever catch up to Ted again. The new trousers Mom had ordered hadn't arrived yet, so the poor guy was wearing high-waters.

Here at camp, birthday breakfast meant waiting in a long line for oatmeal or corn flakes or the rare stack of pancakes. Mitsi, wearing her getas, huddled up with Mom and Obaachan under their one umbrella, out of the drizzle.

There wasn't a birthday candle in sight, but Mitsi made a wish anyway. She wished that the whole family would find seats together. And her wish came true! She could imagine that they were a normal family again, spooning up oatmeal, sipping tea. Everything was delicious, until Ted said, "May I be excused?"

His friends could wait. It was her birthday after all. But then Debbie appeared at her elbow.

"Here." Ted slid off the bench and pretended to dust off the spot where he'd been sitting. "A throne for you, m'lady."

Debbie giggled. "Thank you, gallant sir." She scooted onto the seat and handed Mitsi a small paper sack, the edges rolled over to keep it closed. "Happy birthday."

"Thank you." Mitsi opened it. "Penny candy!"

"One piece for each year."

Mitsi pulled out two BB Bats. "Which flavor do you want?"

"They're for you," Debbie said.

Mitsi jiggled the suckers up and down. "Strawberry or banana."

"Banana." Debbie took the sucker and began to unwrap it.

"For breakfast?" Mom made a face.

"It's a special day." Pop reached for his coffee cup.

Mitsi unwrapped her sucker, too, and took a lick. If she closed her eyes, she could pretend she was eating a strawberry fresh from the plant on Uncle Shig's farm.

"Do you want to go see if you got any mail today?" Debbie stuck out her tongue. "Is it yellow?"

"No." Mitsi stuck hers out, too. "Red?"

Debbie shook her head. "Nope. Keep licking. So do you want to?"

Mitsi hated to miss a day working at the gate. She was getting closer to that three dollars and ninety-five cents. But a birthday was a day to celebrate. To have some fun. Mitsi glanced at her parents. "May I be excused?"

"You're the birthday girl." Mom winked. "I guess whatever you want, goes."

The girls slid off the bench and headed for the front door, past Ted and his friends.

"Where are you going?" Lefty asked.

Mitsi glanced at Debbie.

"None of your beeswax!" Debbie grabbed Mitsi's arm and they ran outside and down the way. They collapsed against the back of the laundry house. "We told them," Debbie said, laughing.

"*You* told them," Mitsi said. Something caught her eye over Debbie's shoulder. "Hey, they're after us!"

The girls took off running, dodging behind barracks and hiding behind garbage cans. At one point, the boys pounded past them as they crouched behind a set of flowered bedsheets hanging on the line in front of Barracks 17. Mitsi covered her mouth to keep the giggles inside.

Debbie peeked around the sheets. "I think the coast is clear." She led the way out of their hiding spot.

Ted and Lefty tore around the corner of the building. "Gotcha!" Ted grabbed Mitsi, and Lefty grabbed Debbie. "Now you're trapped."

Debbie shook Lefty off. "We knew you were back there."

Lefty squinted. "Like heck you did."

Debbie answered by popping her sucker in and out of her mouth. "You guys want to go over to Area D?" she asked.

"I thought we were going to the post office," said Mitsi.

"We can't," Lefty said.

"Not without a pass," Ted added.

"That's what you think." Debbie linked arms with Mitsi. "See you later." She started off, with Mitsi scrambling along next to her. "Want to play a trick on them?"

Mitsi grinned. "Sure." They could go to the post office later.

Debbie stopped and turned around. "I bet you a nickel we get in."

"I'll take that bet," Lefty said.

She held out her hand. "Let's see the nickel."

Lefty held his hand out to Ted. "Give her a nickel."

Ted patted his pockets. "I'm busted flat. Can't help."

Disgusted, Lefty reached into his own pocket. "Here." He held out the coin. "Where's yours?"

She fished one out of her pocket, too. "Right here. Come on."

Like the animals boarding Noah's ark, they walked two by two, girls in front, boys right behind. Pudge ran up, stopping them. "What are you doing?"

Lefty jerked his thumb at Debbie. "She says she's going over to Area D."

Pudge gave Debbie an admiring glance. "The Ferris wheel's over there," he said. "Course, we can't ride it."

"Just like we can't get into Area D," Ted predicted.

"We'll see about that." Debbie lowered her voice to a whisper. "They changed the rules last night. My mom was there, taking dictation." She stood up straight again. "How are we going to spend our ten cents?" she said, loud enough for the boys to hear.

"I wonder how we're going to spend ours," Lefty countered. They bickered back and forth all the way to the gate between Area A and Area D. Debbie marched right up to the soldiers standing guard, as if they were carrying croquet mallets instead of guns.

"My friends and I want to go over there," she said, pointing. "To run on the racetrack."

The soldier closest to her scratched his nose. "'Fraid we can't let you," he said. "You need a pass." He looked at the getas on Mitsi's feet. "Besides, how would you run in those?"

"Ha!" Lefty stuck out his hand. "Pay up."

Debbie tilted her nose in the air. Mitsi followed suit. "Sir, would you mind checking on that?"

The soldier stopped chewing his gum. "You want me to check on that?"

Debbie nodded. Mitsi did, too, even though her palms were sweaty.

The soldier's partner tapped him with the butt of his rifle. "Aw, go on. Ask."

The first soldier headed inside the tiny guardhouse. Mitsi saw him pick up a receiver. He seemed to be talking to someone. She held her breath when she saw him walk back their way.

"What do you know?" The solider scratched up under his helmet. "The sarge says it's okay. They don't need a pass anymore."

The second soldier reached over the top of the gate and unlocked it. It swung open. "Be our guest." He waved the kids through.

On the other side, Debbie thrust her hand at Lefty. "Pay up."

"Make me." He glowered.

Ted jabbed him in the side. "Don't be a welcher."

"What kind of friend are you?" Lefty asked Ted. But he handed over the coin.

"The kind who can't wait to run that track!" Ted loped off. Lefty spun around to follow, with Pudge puffing behind.

"I can't really run in these," Mitsi apologized.

"That's okay." Debbie wrapped her arm around Mitsi's. "The boys were giving me a headache, anyway."

They started off around the oval track. "Did you ever come to the fair here?" Debbie asked.

"When I was little." Mitsi took an extra-big step to avoid a puddle. "I only remember the scones."

"I came with my dad once. We watched a horse race." Debbie's voice softened. "I picked the prettiest horse. Black, with a pure white stripe down its nose. And he won!" She smiled at the memory. "I got a pink cotton candy to celebrate."

"He sounds like a nice dad," Mitsi said.

"Hey." Debbie tugged on her arm. "It's true."

Mitsi looked to where Debbie was pointing. There *were* people living in the horse stalls.

"Maybe we don't have it so bad," Debbie said.

Mitsi got a funny feeling in her stomach. As if she'd eaten about a pound of penny candy, instead of one sucker. "Yeah."

They were quiet for a bit, trying not to stare into the horse-stall rooms, even though many of the doors were standing open. Probably to air them out.

"I want to go back." Mitsi almost said, "Back home." Those slipshod, splintery barracks certainly weren't like home, but they were more like a home than a horse stall.

The nice guard waved at them as they crossed back into Area A.

Mitsi offered him a piece of candy from her bag. He chose a Tootsie Roll.

"See you next time," he called.

Debbie didn't say a word the entire walk to the post office. Mitsi had never seen her quiet for that long. Was she thinking about those people living in horse stalls, too? Or was she thinking about her father?

Debbie pulled a nickel from her pocket. "Here." She handed it to Mitsi. "Your share of the bet."

"It was your bet," Mitsi said.

Debbie pushed the money on her. "I don't want it." She crossed the path toward the post office. "I don't want to go over there anymore."

"Me, either." Mitsi pulled open the door, and Debbie followed her inside.

"My two favorite customers!" Mel grinned when he saw them.

Mitsi offered him a piece of candy.

"Oh, I can't resist these." He pulled out a root beer barrel, unwrapped it, and popped it in his mouth. "Give me a second and I'll see if there's anything for you."

He disappeared for a moment, then was back at the window, holding out two pieces of mail. One was a card for Mitsi; she now knew that handwriting by heart. The other was a small envelope, with a lot of official-looking writing. It looked like the return address was stamped Montana.

"Miyake, right?" His forehead wrinkled. "A-50-2?"

Debbie folded the envelope and shoved it into her pocket. She put on a smile and pointed at Mitsi's mail. "Looks like Dash sent you a birthday card."

Mitsi opened it up. There was a letter tucked in, too, but she'd save that for later. The front of the card was a drawing of a dog, looking droopy. Inside, the card said, *It's "ruff" not to spend your special day with you.* Underneath that, Mrs. Bowker had written, *Dash and I both send warm birthday wishes. He says he is saving a bone for you.*

"That's cute." Debbie tossed her sucker stick into the trash. "Hey, I better get going."

"I'll walk you." Mitsi slid the birthday card back into the envelope.

"Naw. It's okay." Debbie bolted for the door and ran outside.

Mitsi was so surprised, she couldn't move. Had she said something wrong? Done something wrong? Or was it something to do with that letter Debbie had gotten? Mitsi puzzled it over as she walked home.

After supper, Mom reached behind the blanket that hung between Ted's cot and hers and brought out a pan of store-bought cinnamon rolls. Three mismatched birthday candles were poked into the top.

"We have to wait for Ted," Mitsi said.

As if on cue, her brother slipped through the door. "Gotcha something, sis." He tossed her one of those brand-new Archie comic books. "Happy birthday!"

Ted was supposed to be busted flat. Where'd he get the money for a comic book?

"Ready to make a wish?" Mom asked.

Pop lit the three candles, and Mitsi got her second "Happy Birthday" serenade of the day.

"How did you manage this?" Mitsi inhaled the sweet cinnamon smell of the rolls.

"You know all those people that hang around the gate?" Pop asked. "Your mom got some teenager to go to the store across from the camp. She sent him for a birthday cake, but this was the best he could do."

It was kind of funny that both Mom and Mitsi were making good use of that fence, without either of them knowing what the other was doing. Mitsi looked at her brother and thought about changing her wish. Maybe he hadn't wanted to give Lefty the money for the bet. So he'd have something to buy her a gift. That was probably it. She inhaled and then blew out the candles.

"Your wish will come true." Obaachan served Mitsi a roll balanced on a paper napkin.

"Big deal," said Ted. "There were only three candles."

Mitsi ate her roll slowly, letting the sweetness fill her mouth, hoping that her wish *would* come true. She could almost feel the cool silver of the chain on her neck, feel the slight weight of the locket at her throat.

"Kind of a funny birthday cake." Mom kissed the top of her head.

Mitsi stopped chewing. "The best I've ever had."

And because it was so delicious, she took the tiniest bites possible until every crumb was gone.

CHAPTER THIRTEEN

The Long Train Ride

Mitsi counted her money. Twice. Finally, she'd earned enough for a locket! She got out a piece of paper to write to Mrs. Bowker. First, she answered the latest letter "from" Dash.

Dear Dash,

I'm sorry you got stung. Maybe that will teach you not to chase bees!

I know you asked me to send you a drawing. But I'm not doing much art now. I did meet a guy named Eddie Sato who's a good artist. He was drawing the laundry room on a hot day. The door and windows were open. He titled the drawing "Air conditioning." That was pretty funny.

Thank you for the birthday card. It made me laugh! I had a cinnamon roll birthday cake. Kind of different for a cake, but it tasted great.

I'm here by myself for a change. It's hard to be

*alone here. Even if you go to the bathroom late at
night, you'll run into someone. The reason I'm
alone is that Mom and Pop are at a big meeting and Obaachan and Ted are off with their
friends.*

Mitsi was happy that her grandmother had the
dried-plum ladies to knit and drink tea with. But
she wished Ted would find some better friends.
Anybody besides Lefty.

*Well, I guess that's all for now. I'll tell Debbie
you said hello. I mean, woof.*
Love, Mitsi

Pretty soon she wasn't going to have to imagine
having Dash around — he would be around. At least
around her neck, in the locket. She couldn't wait.

Mitsi took out a second piece of paper and began
writing.

Dear Mrs. Bowker,
*You're already doing me a big favor by keeping
Dash. Could I ask for one more? I thought of a way*

to have him at camp — a picture locket. I think you
can buy one for $3.95 (money enclosed) at Sears,
Roebuck. Would you do that for me and send it here?

   Thank you so much!
   Love,
   Mitsi

She put her money in the envelope along with the letters and pasted on a stamp. If she hurried, it might get out in today's mail. She jumped off the stoop and jogged over to Debbie's, but there wasn't any answer to her knock.

Lefty was hanging around outside the canteen. He sniffed the air when he saw Mitsi. "I thought I smelled something funny," he said.

Mitsi glared at him and went inside. She heard the bell tinkle behind her. Lefty walked over to the candy display.

"Just in time," Mel said as she handed him the letter. "This should be there tomorrow or the next day."

Mitsi counted up in her head. If it took two days for a letter to go to Mrs. Bowker's and back, and a couple more days for Mrs. Bowker to have time to go shopping, she might have her locket in a little more than a week.

"See you later, Mel!" She turned toward the door. A movement across the room caught her eye. Had Lefty put something under his shirt?

"Mel?" Mitsi stopped. "Mel?" He was gone, probably into the back room where he sorted the mail.

Lefty sauntered outside. Mitsi waited another moment for Mel to return. When he didn't, she went outside, too. Lefty was nowhere in sight. She walked toward the main gate and looked around. There he was. By the flagpole.

She marched over to him. "What were you doing in the canteen?"

"It's a free country." His grin was chocolate coated. "I can go in there when I want." He took a step toward her. "Now beat it."

Mitsi beat it, wiping sweaty palms on her skirt. Where did Lefty get that chocolate? She didn't see him buy it. That guy was up to no good.

She found herself walking upstream against a crowd of people filing out of the mess hall. The meeting must be over. And from the looks on the faces she passed, the news must not have been good.

But Mitsi never imagined how bad it could be. When her parents told her, right before supper, she felt sick to her stomach. Mom let her stay back at their room. "I'll bring you some ginger ale and toast," she'd said.

Mitsi crawled across Ted's cot to her own and lay down on her back, holding her stomach. Even though she'd counted all the knots up on the ceiling a dozen times before, she counted them again: fifteen, sixteen, seventeen. That last one was the one shaped like a dog, with perky ears and a little flag of a tail, like Dash's. She rolled onto her side, the hay crinkling in the mattress as she moved, and cuddled Chubby Bear close, stroking him as if he were Dash.

She felt all twitchy, like when she had the chicken pox that time. Only this feeling was inside her, in a place that couldn't be soothed by calamine lotion. She needed to get the news out of her head.

Mitsi shifted upright, set Chubby Bear aside, then fluffed her pillow and set it behind her back. She picked up her stationery pad and pen and started a letter. Instead of writing "Dear Mrs. Bowker," she wrote "Dear Dash." She knew he wasn't going to read it, of course. She knew it was Mrs. Bowker who was writing to her. But Dash had always been there when Mitsi was sad. He was her best friend. It was a comfort to imagine talking to him.

When I heard Mom and Pop say that we were moving, I thought that meant we'd get to come back home. But it doesn't. We're going to another camp, called Minidoka. It's pretty far away, in Idaho. Pop says it's a three-day train ride.

Mitsi's arms got itchier when she wrote those words. She knew there was nothing, really, on her skin, but she put the pen down and scratched like crazy until the feeling passed. Then she finished her letter:

I'll write as soon as I get there so you have our new address.
Love, Mitsi
PS Tell Mrs. Bowker I hope she hasn't mailed the locket yet. I won't be here to get it.

. . .

Two days later, Mitsi and her family finished packing up all of their belongings. Again.

Some rusty, musty train cars had been put back into service for the ride to Minidoka. One of the churches in Seattle sent decks of cards and coloring books for the children. "To help pass the time," said the lady who gave Mitsi a coloring book. Mitsi thanked her but gave it away to the first little kid she saw.

Mitsi woke up, not to Mom's voice but to a pounding on the door. She practically levitated out of bed. Pop fumbled his way to answer it, tripping over Ted's cot. The clock on his nightstand said four.

"Collecting the bedding." A worker ducked his head as he stood on the stoop, as if embarrassed to be there so early in the morning. "Breakfast is in an hour." He waited while Mom turned into a tornado, whirling around the room, stripping sheets and blankets from the five cots.

They dressed quickly, pulling on clothes laid out the night before. It was so early, Mitsi felt a bit queasy.

"You'll feel better after you eat something," Pop told her.

Mitsi couldn't imagine eating, but the good smells — good smells! — that danced around her as she waited in the mess hall line set her stomach to growling. When her turn came, she took a plate loaded with ham and eggs, toast, fried potatoes, and an orange. They'd never been served such a breakfast. She ate every bite, pocketing the orange for later.

A little before seven, sleepy and full, Mitsi leaned against Pop as they waited at the loading point. She counted eleven passenger cars, two dining cars, two baggage cars, and a pair of Pullman sleepers hooked on behind the engine. Each car looked shabbier and sadder than the one in front of it.

Soon, soldiers started calling out orders, and by seven thirty, Mitsi and her family were on the train. MPs patrolled the aisles, asking people to sit down. Mom took out her handkerchief, cleaning a seat for Obaachan. When she finished, her hanky was gray with dirt.

Though it was sweltering when they boarded, the MPs closed all the windows and drew down all the shades. Ted said it was because some people had thrown rocks and eggs at the first train to leave the week before. Mitsi felt like she was suffocating. Obaachan, her face chalky from the heat, fanned herself with a religious pamphlet someone had handed out. Mom found the toilet and washed out her hanky. She brought it back, damp. "It's just a closet," she reported, with a shake of her head. She draped the hanky on Obaachan's neck to help cool her off. Pop and Ted went out to stand on the platform between the train cars until the MPs shooed them back inside.

"This stinks." Ted flopped onto the seat opposite Mitsi.

"It really does." Mitsi held the orange to her nose. The passenger compartment smelled like a big pail of dirty baby diapers left out in the sun. When the engine jerked into motion and began pulling the seventeen cars down the track, a tiny bit of fresh air snaked its way into their compartment. After several hours, when they were out in the middle of nowhere, the MPs gave the okay to open the shades.

Mitsi pressed her nose to the grimy window to look at the passing scenery. Everything was brown.

Different shades of brown, like the rust in the train bathroom, or the murky cup of coffee Pop tried to drink, or the deep chocolate of the Hershey bar that one MP was munching on. But brown all the same. It made her feel even hotter.

She turned away from the window and rummaged in her book bag, pulling out paper and pencil.

Wednesday, August 19
Dear Dash,

If my handwriting looks bumpy, it's because I'm writing on a train. The movies make train travel seem so luxurious. But it's hot and smelly and we're going to have to sleep sitting up in our seats. There are only two Pullman cars, but they're for the moms with little kids.

We do get to eat our meals in the dining car. Ted said he heard there are ice-cream sundaes for dessert. I hope that's true. I haven't had ice cream since forever.

I wonder what's blooming in Mrs. Bowker's garden. Write and tell me! And it's okay by me if you take her to our special patch of blackberries. I don't think I'll be back in time to pick any.

Mitsi leaned back against the seat, remembering last August, picking blackberries with Dash. Somehow, he could wriggle around the sharp thorns, like a rabbit. He would vacuum ripe berries off the vines while Mitsi picked, filling coffee cans that she'd fitted out with wire handles. She closed her eyes and could almost taste blackberry pie.

Mitsi felt a tap on her shoulder. She opened her eyes and saw Debbie.

"Hey."

Mitsi wiggled her fingers in a wave. "Hey, back at you." She hadn't seen much of Debbie since her birthday. Right afterward, Debbie's mom got sick and they'd been taking most of their meals in their room. Mitsi had seen Debbie carrying a tray once or twice. They'd visit for just a minute before Debbie would say, "Well, I better get back to my mom." She hadn't even come out when the Seattle library sent a bunch of books for the camp.

"We're in the next car up." Debbie fingered the torn upholstery on the back of Mitsi's seat. "I thought the scenery might be better back here."

"Really?" Mitsi wondered how the scenery could improve between cars.

"No, you goof." Debbie nudged onto the seat with Mitsi. "That was a joke."

Ted hopped up. "You can sit here. I'm going to go look for Lefty."

"Behave yourself," Mom said without looking up from the *Ladies' Home Journal* article she was reading: "How Should Children Be Trained for a War Situation?" Obaachan was snoring softly in the seat next to her.

Debbie didn't take Ted's spot. "Do you want to go exploring?"

"Can I?" Mitsi addressed the top of her mother's head, which was still bent over the magazine. "I mean, may I?"

"Be back in half an hour," said Mom.

"And we'll behave ourselves." Debbie giggled.

Debbie was like a kitten, poking here, sniffing there, and pouncing on anything new and different.

"Look!" She dragged Mitsi to the window. A heron stood on one leg in a rocky riverbed, calmly eying the rushing water for his fish dinner. Farther on, they spied a pair of long-eared jackrabbits scampering in the sagebrush, kicking up dust devils with their powerful back legs. "I hope no fox gets them," Mitsi said.

"Or bobcat," added Debbie.

"Are there bobcats out here?" Mitsi had only ever seen one, at the Woodland Park Zoo.

Debbie shrugged. "It sure looks like there could be."

Mitsi watched the passing scenery more carefully after that. When it was suppertime, Debbie had to go rejoin her mother. Mitsi ate with her own family in the dining car. The roast beef was tasty, but she kept waiting for that ice-cream sundae that never appeared. Back in their car, Mitsi watched the setting sun paint the hills purple and burnish the river to a glowing gold. But as fiercely as she watched, she didn't see as much as one tuft of a bobcat's ear.

When the sky was inky dark, Debbie returned to their car, carrying a blanket.

"Mom says I can spend the night here," she said. "If it's okay with you, Mrs. Kashino."

Mom rearranged things so the girls could sleep next to one another.

Obaachan tucked the blanket around them and they snuggled up on the train seats.

"This is our first sleepover," Mitsi said. The seat was lumpy. And musty. "I don't think there's going to be much sleeping."

"There never is at a sleepover!" Debbie smoothed the blanket over her lap. "Let's play I spy. I'll go first. I spy with my little eye something that is round."

"Is it Ted's head?" Mitsi guessed.

"Hey!" Ted stretched his leg out to give her a kick.

Debbie giggled. "No."

Mitsi made some more guesses. "No, no, no," said Debbie.

"Are you sure this is something in this train car?" Mitsi asked.

Debbie crossed her heart. "Scout's honor."

Mitsi looked around for something else to guess. "The bolt on the window?"

"Bingo!" Debbie slapped her hands together. "Your turn."

Around them, people began to fall asleep. Mom put her finger to her lips to signal to the girls that they needed to be quieter. Mitsi leaned closer to Debbie and whispered, "I spy with my little eye something that is blue."

Debbie touched her nose. "My glasses!"

Mom had dozed off. She gave out a long snore. Both girls giggled.

"I made it too easy," Mitsi said.

Pop snored, too, and the girls had to duck under their blankets to stifle their giggles. Mitsi couldn't see Debbie, but she could still hear her.

"He sounds like a bear!" Debbie said.

Pop snorted and Mitsi giggled harder.

Debbie's giggles stopped. "My dad snores, too. Just as loud."

Being under the blanket made Mitsi braver. "Where is he?"

Debbie didn't change the subject this time, as she had before. Her voice grew quiet. "Someplace else."

"Is he —" Mitsi wasn't sure how to ask the question that popped into her mind. "I mean, what's his name?"

"James. James Miyake." Debbie shifted on the seat. "I'm pretty tired." She curled up, away from Mitsi. "See you in the morning."

Mitsi couldn't sleep. She wanted to know about Debbie's dad. Was he even alive? Is that why just saying his name seemed to make her so sad? She had a million questions, but instead of asking even one of them, all she said was, "Sleep tight."

Thursday, August 20
Dear Dash,

I dreamt last night that you were sleeping next to me. When I woke up, and you weren't there, I started to cry. I told Debbie about it. She said she'd had a bad dream, too, and that we were in the "doldrums" and needed to find an antidote. We made a scavenger hunt on the train, looking for one. Nobody seemed to know what we were talking about. But one lady thought some raisins might help. We took them even though we both think they're disgusting. Someone's big sister sprayed us with her Shalimar perfume. And one of the soldiers even gave us a pack of Clove gum — my favorite. We shared with Ted and Lefty. It was funny. We never found the antidote, but I ended up feeling better. Debbie did, too.

I still miss you. But it helps having a friend like Debbie.

. . .

Over the next day and a half, Mitsi added to the letter to Dash. She wrote about getting that promised ice-cream sundae after supper the second night. She wrote about banging her elbows while trying to wash up in the teeny-tiny train sink. And about playing hide-and-seek with Debbie in the baggage car until that grouchy MP kicked them out. She kept writing because there was no way to mail anything along the way. It turned into a very, very long letter.

Near the end of the third day, the train chugged to a stop in the middle of a desert. "Everybody off," called the MPs. Mitsi grabbed her things and climbed down the steps, groaning and stretching and gasping at the heat. She hadn't even worked out the kinks in her legs before the MPs were shouting orders again. "This way, folks."

Mitsi followed her family as they were loaded onto yellow buses with SUN VALLEY painted on the side. The buses were as hot as the train, but the seats weren't so lumpy. Mitsi looked around. Debbie and her mom must've gotten on a different bus.

Though there was nothing but sand and sagebrush outside, Mitsi stared out the window the entire ride. When the parade of buses stopped, she looked around. "Are we here?"

Her parents stood to gather their belongings. "It appears so," said Pop.

Mitsi leaned toward the window for a last peek. She couldn't see the camp. She couldn't see anything through the dirty haze.

She wobbled off the bus, battling a rocking sensation, as if she was still on the train. The small group of people that had come out to greet the buses looked like they'd been rolled in talcum powder.

It didn't take long before Mitsi and her family looked the same way. Each step sent a puff of dust billowing up from the ground. The white feather on Pop's fedora turned brown. Obaachan couldn't stop coughing. It was Camp Harmony all over again: Lines to get checked in. Lines to get their apartment assignment. Lines to use the latrines. Finally, they got through all the lines and found their apartment. Just like at Camp Harmony, the only furnishings were five cots — this time with real mattresses — and a potbelly stove. All the furniture

Pop had made had been left behind. They were starting over from scratch.

The floor was so thick with fine dust that Mitsi left footprints as she brought her things inside. She plunked down on the closest of the grimy cots to finish her letter to Dash. In wobbly letters, she wrote:

> *We are in block three and Debbie is right next door. That is the only good thing about this place.*
>
> *The only good thing.*

CHAPTER FOURTEEN

Vitamin D

Mitsi's throat was raw from the dust, and the ringing in her ears was driving her crazy. Mom heard from Mrs. Suda who heard from Mrs. Kusakabe that the ringing was because of the altitude.

"Seattle is only about five hundred feet above sea level," Pop explained. "Here, we're about four thousand feet above. That's a big difference."

"As soon as you get used to the altitude, the ringing will stop," Mom promised.

Mitsi rolled over on her cot, blanketed in misery. She was never going to get used to anything about this place, not the dust or the miles of sagebrush or the pancake-flat landscape without one tree to provide shade from the bullying sun.

Through the thin wall, she could hear the Sudas — all nine of them — waking up. The baby, Louise, was howling and Mrs. Suda started singing the Mockingbird song to quiet her. Mitsi pulled her pillow over her head. Yes, please hush, little baby. Don't you cry — some people are trying to sleep!

The pillow did not help. With twenty people crammed into six small apartments in one long, narrow building, quiet was too much to hope for. Adults snored or argued. Kids cried out from bad dreams, or just cried. Even though they were whispered, Mitsi could hear the Suda family's nightly bedtime prayers. Debbie and her mom were on the other side of the Kashinos; they were quiet as mice.

Mitsi propped herself up on her elbow, peering under the blanket that served as the "wall" for the bedroom she shared with Ted and Obaachan. It looked like she was the last one out of bed.

She peeked under her cot. When no one else was around, she and Debbie had knocked out the knothole in the wall between them, and then scraped at the hole with spoons until it was large enough to pass notes through. Mitsi felt around on the floor. No note this morning.

She sat up, bumping her head on the orange crate Pop had nailed above her bed. Until he could gather enough scrap wood to build something, this crate was her dresser.

Mitsi slipped out of her nightie and into some shorts and a top. As she dressed, she whacked her elbow on the potbelly stove, the only other object that had been in the room when they arrived. There wasn't any coal to burn in it, but with temperatures in the hundreds, just looking at it made her hot.

Mitsi rubbed her sore elbow, inspecting for a bruise. Her sneakers *scritch-scratch*ed across the floor. All the buildings had been set up on little stilts to keep them out of the dust, a plan that failed dismally. The gritty stuff got sucked up through the floors no matter how many rags and newspapers Mom stuffed in the cracks.

Debbie was coming out of her apartment, too. "Can I sit with you?" she asked. "Mom's got another headache."

At least it wasn't as far to the mess hall as it had been at Camp Harmony; they only had to walk across a wide path for meals. There were twelve barracks in each of the forty-two blocks, six on a side, all in a row. Each block felt like its own little neighborhood. In between and running perpendicular to the two rows of barracks sat a pair of buildings. One was the combined laundry and bathroom. The other was the mess hall. "Bathroom" was a joke; there was no running water yet in camp. Everyone was using latrines. Ten holers, five holes on a side and absolutely no privacy. Mitsi had been keeping her eye out for boxes.

After she got her breakfast, Mitsi scanned the room. She saw Mom, Pop, and Obaachan. They waved the girls over.

"Where's Ted?" Mitsi asked. Since they'd come to this camp, it was almost as if she didn't have a brother. Mom and Pop let him do whatever he wanted.

"He finished already," Mom said.

"Yum, corn flakes." Debbie took a big spoonful. "I was getting sick of oatmeal."

Mitsi studied her own cereal bowl. Instead of being sprinkled with sugar, it was sprinkled with fine sand. She carefully scooped out a bite, hoping to avoid spooning up any dust. But the minute she started chewing, she could feel the grit on her teeth. She dropped her spoon.

"Eat your breakfast, honey," Mom said. "You already need a belt to hold your shorts up."

Mitsi took another bite, to make Mom happy, even though it was like chewing a mouthful of sandpaper. She wouldn't have any teeth by the time they left camp; they'd all be ground away to nubbins. Pop said it would get better soon, when the seasons changed. Mitsi sure hoped he was right.

Mrs. Suda stopped by their table, balancing Louise on her hip. "The latest word is that school's going to open on October first."

"Not till then?" Mom played peek-a-boo with her napkin. Louise laughed and held her pudgy hands up in front of her own face.

"I hear you." Mrs. Suda clicked her tongue. "Some of those boys have far too much time on their hands. Including my own."

Mitsi glanced at Mom. Was she thinking about Ted? Those looked like new worry wrinkles on her forehead.

"Well, we'd better be going. It's somebody's nap time." Mrs. Suda kissed Louise's plump cheek, then pulled up the bandanna that was tied around the baby's neck. Lots of little kids were walking around the camp looking like outlaws in a Western movie.

It was the only way their mothers could protect them from the ever-blowing dust.

Debbie finished her breakfast. "I should take something to Mother," she said. "Maybe some tea and toast."

"Tell her I have some aspirin if she needs any." Mom picked up her own tray. "Oh, there's Mrs. Iseri. I wanted to ask her about helping with Sunday school."

Pop finished his coffee, then headed out with Mr. Suda to scrounge up more scrap wood. Obaachan joined the dried-plum ladies for another cup of tea.

"Do you want to come with me?" Debbie asked.

Mitsi shrugged. Her family didn't seem to care that they'd left her all by herself. "Okay," she said. "Afterward, maybe we can walk over to Block 6. So I can check for mail." There'd been no letters from Dash since they'd arrived at Minidoka. And no packages from Mrs. Bowker, either.

"Great idea!" Debbie poured some hot tea into a mug and set it on a tray. "Then we can see if they have any Creamsicles in the canteen. Mother said I could buy one today." She patted her pocket. "I have enough for you, too." She slathered margarine on a piece of toast and added it to the tray, covering everything with a napkin to try to keep the dust out. "Okay, let's go."

Mitsi waited outside while Debbie took the tray in to her mom. At Camp Harmony, most of the living areas were the same size. Here, bigger families — like the Sudas — got bigger apartments. Smaller families, like Debbie and her mom, had smaller ones. The Kashinos' apartment here was big enough that Mitsi didn't have to crawl over anyone's cot to get in bed.

From the stoop, she could hear Mrs. Miyake's soft voice, but not what she was saying. Debbie stepped back out, putting something in her pocket before gently closing the rough wooden door behind her. "She's feeling a little better." Debbie sailed off the stoop, kicking up a dust cloud. "Ready to go?"

Mitsi flapped her hand in front of her face, trying not to cough.

They walked slowly, seeking out every sliver of shade. The heat might have been bearable if there were a lake or a pool. A canal ran alongside the camp, but it wasn't safe for swimming.

Up ahead, Mr. Hirai was dragging a huge piece of tumbleweed, his shirt soaked with sweat. "Need a hand?" Mitsi called. He waited for them to catch up. They carried the prickly dried shrub back to his barracks.

"May I ask another favor?" When they nodded, he handed them two short brooms made of straw.

"Sweep out a nice, flat spot," he told them. While the girls swept — with gentle motions so as not to stir up too much dust — Mr. Hirai placed several large stones in a design. He'd already made a "river" of smaller ones, curving around more tumbleweed plants.

Mitsi had never thought of tumbleweed as anything but a dirty jumble of twigs. But Mr. Hirai had created something that reminded her of Obaachan's bonsai — delicate forests growing in small dishes — only a hundred times bigger.

"It's beautiful." Mitsi tugged on the neck of her blouse to try to cool off.

"Oh, not as nice as my flower garden at home." Mr. Hirai wiped his forehead with the back of his hand. "But if you look with your heart, you can find beauty anywhere."

They finished their task and watched Mr. Hirai place the new piece of tumbleweed. "There?" he asked them.

"Maybe a little to the left," Mitsi suggested.

He moved it, stepped back, and studied the new layout. "You have a good eye. That's just where it should go," he said.

"Do you need us to do anything else?" Mitsi asked.

"No, you've done enough. Thanks. Where are you headed?"

"To the canteen." Mitsi held up an envelope. "To mail a letter."

"And get a Creamsicle before they're all gone," added Debbie. Two days in a row, the canteen had run out of ice-cream bars. Popsicles, too.

"Canteen, eh?" Mr. Hirai pulled a quarter from his pocket. "Would you please bring me back a Nehi?" He wiped his forehead again. "Any flavor. Just nice and cold."

Mitsi took the quarter. "Okay. See you in a bit."

They passed Mrs. Tokuda's apartment in the next block.

"I was hoping to see you two," she called. She offered them ten cents apiece to watch little Davy the next day. "I've volunteered to type up the new camp newsletter, *The Minidoka Irrigator.* I can take Donna with me; she'll nap. But Davy . . ." She didn't need to say any more. Everybody in their block knew about Davy. Mom called him a pistol.

"Oh, that's okay," Mitsi said. "You don't have to pay us." That's what Mom would want her to say.

Mrs. Tokuda shook her head. "Your family is already doing so much for me." Pop and Mr. Suda had been meeting with the camp superintendent to try to get Mr. Tokuda out of Fort Missoula. Mr. Iseri, too. "Your father won't let me do anything to thank him for all his help. You have to let me pay you."

"Sure," Debbie said. "No problem!" Under her breath to Mitsi she said, "More Creamsicles!" She blew at her bangs, which, like Mitsi's, were glued to her forehead with sweat. "I am so tired of being hot. I'd like to *be* a Creamsicle!" She blew again.

Mitsi agreed. "Or a root beer float." Trickles of sweat bumped down her backbone. "Or a —"

"Stop!" Debbie covered her ears. "This is making me hotter, not cooler."

They played hink pink the rest of the way to the store, which was where the temporary post office was. Mitsi didn't know where Mel ended up, but he wasn't working behind the post office counter anymore.

The new man wore a frown and a name tag that said JOHNSON. He didn't even look up when Mitsi stepped to the counter. She cleared her throat. "Do you have anything for Mitsue Kashino?" She gave him their Minidoka address.

Mr. Johnson looked annoyed, but he did shuffle through a big bin marked with Mitsi's barracks number. "Here you go." He flipped a letter to her.

"Thank you." Mitsi went over to the freezer case to pick out her ice cream and Mr. Hirai's Nehi. "Should I get him grape?" she asked Debbie. But there wasn't an answer. She looked around and saw Debbie handing two envelopes to Mr. Johnson. Mitsi wondered who they were to.

"Grape for Mr. Hirai?" she asked again. Debbie was at her elbow now.

"That's the best flavor." Debbie opened the freezer case and pulled out her selection. On their way outside to eat their treats, the girls bumped into Ted and Lefty and Pudge coming in.

"Oh, look," said Lefty. "It's Mutt and Jeff."

"Oh, that is so funny, I forgot to laugh," Debbie said.

Mitsi stuck her tongue out. "I don't get why Ted likes those guys."

Debbie peeled the paper off her ice cream. "Me, either." She tossed her garbage, then offered to hold the bottle of Nehi so Mitsi could peel the paper off her Popsicle.

"Oh, shoot!" Mitsi stamped her foot, causing a mini dust storm.

"Watch it!" Debbie spun away to protect her ice cream.

"Sorry." Mitsi flapped at the dust. "But I forgot to mail my letter. I'll be right back." She ran inside, fumbled the letter out of her pocket, and handed it to Mr. Johnson. As she turned to leave, she thought she saw something. She blinked. She did see something. Something that made her heart drop into her stomach.

Ted put a candy bar in his pocket. Then he wandered over to the freezer case, studying the choices before strolling out of the store. Mitsi hurried after him, barely able to breathe. When he got outside, he took off at a trot. Lefty and Pudge were on his tail. They were running so hard, she'd never be able to catch up.

"You look like you've seen a ghost," Debbie said. "Was that Mr. Johnson mean to you or something?"

Mitsi shook her head. She couldn't tell Debbie what happened. Couldn't tell anyone. Except Dash. And he was a thousand miles away. "I guess the heat is really getting to me," she said. "I don't feel like eating this anymore. Do you want it?"

Debbie did. She offered to deliver Mr. Hirai's soda so Mitsi could go lie down. "I hope you feel better soon," Debbie said when they parted company.

Mitsi didn't know how she could feel better. The apartment was empty when she got there, so she curled up on her cot, tears pooling in her eyes. She hated this stupid camp. Why did they have to be here? It was all General DeWitt's fault! He had ruined their family. And Lefty had ruined Ted.

She was wrung out, like a washcloth. The heat and her worry and the tears left her exhausted.

When she rolled over to face the wall, the letter in her pocket rustled. She couldn't read it right now. Not even Dash could make her feel better.

Mitsi tucked her head into the crook of her arm and fell into a restless, sweaty sleep.

CHAPTER FIFTEEN

Stealing Home

Being a spy was harder than it looked in the movies. Ted wasn't that easy to follow. And he'd sprouted eyes in the back of his head. He always seemed to know when Mitsi was on the case.

And it didn't help that he and his friends were Houdinis, disappearing right before her very eyes. She knew they had a secret hideout somewhere, but she hadn't been able to find it. For all her watching, as the days went by, she only caught her brother doing all the Ted things he'd always done. A bit of magic. A bit of baseball. A bit of mischief. Nothing more. Maybe she hadn't really seen him take anything at the canteen. A person was innocent until proven guilty. Wasn't that the American way?

One night, Mom and Pop went to yet another meeting. This one was about getting the coal shipment before winter hit. So far, there wasn't one bit of fuel for the hundreds of potbelly stoves in the camp. It was too hot to even think about a stove, but Pop said high deserts get plenty cold in winter. That there'd even be snow. Anything would be better than the mud.

Obaachan was knitting with the dried-plum ladies. Socks for the Red Cross. For the soldiers. Mitsi had the apartment to herself. For once, baby Louise wasn't bawling and Mitsi could actually concentrate on *Thimble Summer*, the book she'd borrowed from Debbie. Garnet and her friend, Citronella, were so busy reading that they got themselves locked up in the public library. And on a Friday night! No one would come until Monday. And the story took place in the olden days, before telephones and electric lights. Scared and hungry, the girls searched the librarian's desk. They shared a candy bar they found, reasoning that they could buy another one when they got out. If they got out.

Mitsi's body was sitting cross-legged on her cot, but her mind was in that dark and creepy library with Garnet and Citronella. When someone began pounding on the library door, her own door slammed open. Mitsi screamed.

"I thought you'd be at the movie." Ted plunked on his cot, untying his shoes. "With Debbie."

"Her mom's not feeling good again." Mitsi sniffed. "You smell like cigarettes." Worry gnawed at her stomach like a rat.

"Aw, it's just the old guys smoking in the ten holer." Ted waved his hand in front of his face. "To cover up the stink."

The women's bathroom smelled pretty bad. Mitsi could only imagine what the men's smelled like.

Ted kicked his shoes under his cot and flopped back. "What're you reading?"

Mitsi shrugged. "Something I borrowed from Debbie." She glanced down at the page in her lap. An idea pushed its way into her brain. "It's about a girl who takes something that doesn't belong to her." She floated the words out like fishing bait. "A candy bar." Maybe she could get Ted to confess.

Ted lay very still on his cot. Finally, he said, "Does she get in trouble?"

"I don't know yet. I haven't read that far." Mitsi flipped a page.

He rolled away, facing the wall. "Sounds like a dumb book." He pulled the pillow over his head.

"Ted?" Mitsi leaned forward on her cot, toward her brother. "Ted?"

"Trying to sleep here!" He yanked the covers over his head, too.

Mitsi finished the chapter. Garnet and her friend were rescued and fed fried egg sandwiches since they missed supper by getting locked in. Mitsi closed the book, then she lay down, too. Ted was right. It was kind of a dumb book. Everything always turned out peachy for Garnet. That's not the way it was in real life.

A scrabbling noise awakened her the next morning. There were enough snakes around that mice weren't a problem, but she still tensed up a bit when she peered under her cot. It wasn't a mouse but a note from Debbie.

Walk with me to the post office?

Usually, it was Mitsi who couldn't wait to go to the post office. But she'd been so distracted about Ted that she hadn't gone in days. Yawning, she grabbed a pencil and wrote her answer on the back.

Okay.

She bolted down some corn flakes in the dining hall, then ran back to their apartment. Pop was wrestling a desk inside. "What do you think about this?" he asked. "Mr. Suda and I are going to make one for Debbie, too."

Mitsi ran her hands across the top. "It's perfect." Somehow, Pop had sanded the rough wood so smooth that her fingers couldn't find the tiniest of splinters.

"Okay if I put it here?" He wedged the desk next to Mitsi's cot.

She tested the pencil drawer. It wouldn't open. "The drawer's stuck."

Pop jiggled it all the way out, then rubbed the bottom sliders with a bar of Ivory soap. "This should do the trick." He replaced the drawer and it slid right in and out again.

"Smooth as silk," Mitsi said.

"Now all you need is some homework." Pop winked. "Only a couple more weeks."

Mitsi opened the pencil drawer and put her writing materials inside. Everyone else in the family seemed to have found plenty to do to fill the hot, dusty days. Mom organized the Sunday school and was teaching craft classes. Last week, it had been felt animal pins. Mitsi had made a tan dog, like Dash, that was pinned to her blouse. Obaachan taught ikebana. Of course, there were no flowers in camp, but she could make tumbleweed arrangements look beautiful. If Pop wasn't out hunting for scrap lumber, he was building furniture. He'd made two chests of drawers, five chairs, and now Mitsi's desk. And, when he wasn't hanging out with Lefty and Pudge, Ted delivered the camp newsletter.

Debbie popped through the door.

"Come see what Pop made!" Mitsi showed it off, sliding the pencil drawer in and out.

Pop smiled at Debbie. "We're making one for you, too." He bent over to examine some invisible flaw on the desktop. "You'll have it before school starts."

Debbie tapped the desktop with her fingers. "Thank you, Mr. Kashino."

"We're going to the post office," Mitsi told him. "And then we're babysitting for Davy."

Pop nodded absently, already at work on Debbie's desk.

Clouds of dust ballooned after each step she and

Debbie took. Mitsi coughed. "I'll be so glad when winter comes," she said. Debbie only nodded. Mitsi was used to this. Anything to do with fathers turned her quiet. Sad. Mitsi wasn't sure why, but she knew Debbie well enough now to let it be. It was like a freckle or a chipped tooth or a cowlick, a part of who she was.

When they got to the post office, Debbie pulled out an envelope. She kissed it for luck. "It's got to work this time." She pushed it through the brass slot.

"What do you mean?"

Debbie ran her fingers along the mail counter. Mean Mr. Johnson was nowhere in sight. "I guess it's okay to tell you. 'Cause of what your dad's doing." She lowered her voice and pulled Mitsi behind a war bonds display. "You know where Mrs. Iseri's husband is? And Mrs. Tokuda's?"

Mitsi nodded. "Fort Missoula."

"My dad's there, too."

Mitsi felt an odd rush of relief. "So he's not dead."

"He was president of the Japanese Chamber of Commerce. They took him away after Pearl Harbor. In his pajamas."

"It was raining when they took Mr. Iseri and he didn't even have a hat." Mitsi remembered that sad day.

"I never got to see him after that." Debbie pressed on her eyelids.

And Mitsi had thought it was hard not seeing Dash. "I'm really sorry."

"I have a photo that I keep under my pillow." Debbie pulled her hands away from her face. "Sometimes I pretend he's there, tucking me in."

"So *what's* got to work?" Mitsi asked.

Debbie looked confused. "I don't get it."

"That letter." Mitsi pointed to the mail slot. "You said it had to work this time."

Debbie sighed. "Mom hired a lawyer. He said to get references from people who would swear that Dad wasn't a spy. So she did. Five of them, including one from Reverend Andrews and one from Father Tibesar."

"Everybody loves them," Mitsi said.

Debbie's mouth curved into a small smile. "They have God on their side, right?"

"Right!"

"Plus, what your dad and Mr. Suda are doing. Mom says it might make all the difference."

"Pop is really smart." Mitsi thought about all the furniture he was making out of bits of scrap wood. How he had used a plain old bar of soap to fix a sticky drawer. "He can fix anything."

Debbie took off her glasses and brushed her eyes. "You're an awful good listener."

"I had a good teacher." Mitsi straightened a poster on the post office wall, trying not to think about Dash. The poster said FOOD IS A WEAPON. DON'T WASTE IT. She gave the corner a final tap. "We're going to be late. Come on!"

Mrs. Tokuda had Donna all bundled up when they got there. "I shouldn't be more than an hour." She bent to kiss Davy good-bye. "Bye, sweetheart." She hurried off, with the baby in her arms.

"I not sweetheart. I dog!" Davy romped around the apartment on all fours. "Woof, woof."

"Should we teach this dog some tricks?" Mitsi asked Debbie.

"Woof!" Davy barked, wagging his rear as if he had a tail. "Tricks!"

Mitsi held out a raisin. "Roll over." Davy rolled twice, then barked again. She petted him and fed him the raisin from the palm of her hand. Then he wanted them to take him for a walk, but Mitsi didn't think it was a very good idea to tie the bathrobe belt "leash" around his neck. Debbie found a clothespin and pinned it to his collar. When they went outside, he lifted his leg on Mr. Hirai's tumbleweed.

The girls fell against each other giggling. "Thank goodness for his diapers," Debbie said. That got them laughing all over again.

After his walk, they took him home, getting him cleaned up and turned back into a boy before Mrs. Tokuda returned. She brought a copy of the latest newsletter. Debbie leaned over Mitsi's shoulder as they skimmed the front page.

"Hey, there might be movies next month," Debbie said.

"Did you see this?" Mitsi pointed to an article near the bottom of the page. "It says that two skunks were sighted and killed in Block 41."

"Pee-uw!" Debbie held her nose. "Thank goodness it wasn't in our block."

Mrs. Tokuda paid them each a dime. "Next week, same time?" she asked.

The girls nodded. Mitsi thought about the icy Popsicle she would buy with her share. Banana. She could almost feel the lovely cold in her mouth, dripping down her throat.

Debbie flipped her coin. "Next stop, the canteen!" She must have been thinking the same thing. They walked toward Block 6 as fast as they could manage in the heat; Mitsi felt twin trickles from her armpits to her waist.

"What's going on over there?" Debbie slowed down. "Look at all those people."

A crowd had gathered outside the canteen, and the manager was waving his arms and shouting at one of the camp security guards.

Debbie tugged Mitsi forward and they wiggled around bystanders to get close enough to hear. It didn't take long to figure out there'd been a burglary.

"Not much cash missing," the manager said. "But I'd say they got about fifty bucks' worth of merchandise. Candy bars, playing cards, but mostly cigarettes."

Mitsi couldn't breathe. Candy bars. And cigarettes.

"Canteen's closed, folks," the security guard called out. "Why don't you all head on home."

Debbie groaned. "I really wanted a Creamsicle!"

Mitsi had a bad feeling. "I better see if Pop needs any help," she said.

"Wait up!" Debbie trotted after her.

Mitsi hadn't gone far when someone yanked her pigtails.

"Ouch!" She whipped around.

"You've got a piece of tumbleweed in your hair." Ted held up the evidence.

"Where have you been?"

"Playing ball."

"With Lefty?" Mitsi braced herself for the answer.

"Naw. He's not much for baseball." Ted shrugged. "I've got papers to deliver." He jogged away.

"Were you at the field by the store?" Mitsi called after him.

But he didn't answer.

"Your brother is so nice." Debbie leaned against Mitsi, shaking a rock out of her shoe. "You're lucky."

Mitsi didn't say anything. She didn't feel very lucky right now. She felt worried.

When they reached their barracks, Debbie skipped up the steps to her apartment. "See you at supper!"

Mitsi nodded, then opened her own door, taking a deep breath before stepping inside. *Ted was playing baseball. Ted was playing baseball. Ted was playing baseball.* If she said it enough times, it might be true.

CHAPTER SIXTEEN

A Silver Lining

The camp superintendent stopped by their dining hall at lunchtime a few days later. "I want to update you on the recent burglary case," he said. "We think we'll have it wrapped up in no time. And we don't anticipate any further problems," he added.

Mitsi shot a glance at Ted. He dug into his food as if nothing was wrong. Maybe nothing was wrong. Maybe she'd been worried over nothing. She felt herself relax for the first time in days.

After lunch, Mom took her shopping at the camp store. "I thought we could get you something new for school," Mom said. Mitsi picked out a wool skirt with a matching bolero and some new anklets. Not white, however. Too much mud. She also got a new binder. For a moment, it felt like before the camps, when she and Mom would go school shopping at J.C. Penney.

"Let's check for the mail before we head back," Mom suggested. They waited in line at the window. A lady with a big smile was filling in for Sourpuss Johnson. "Anything for Kashino?" Mom asked when it was their turn.

"Let me see." The lady looked around. "I'm new, so it might take me a minute."

"We're in no hurry." Mom shifted her packages around, before wandering over to the magazine rack. She flipped through a *Ladies' Home Journal.*

"I found a couple of letters for Kashino." The lady handed them over the counter. "Do you think there might be anything else?"

Mom shook her head. "I'm not expecting anything." She put the magazine back on the rack. "Oh, I did order some slacks for my son."

"May I go buy a licorice rope?" Mitsi asked.

Mom opened her pocketbook. "Get a few butterscotch drops for Obaachan, too."

Was she hungry for a licorice rope? Or an Abba-Zaba? What about a Baby Ruth? Abba-Zaba, Mitsi decided. It would last longer. She paid for the candy. Mom was still chatting with the mail lady.

"Look what she found. For you!" Mom took the bag of candy from Mitsi and handed her a small package wrapped in brown paper and tied up with string.

Mitsi untied the string and ripped off the paper to reveal a small blue box. Mitsi took off the lid. "My locket!" It was even prettier than the one she'd seen in the Sears catalog.

"What a lovely gift," Mom said.

"It's not a gift." Mitsi quickly explained. "And now I can keep Dash with me all the time." She handed Mom the wrappings and opened the locket.

There were already two photos inside. One of Mitsi and one of Dash. "I wonder how Mrs. Bowker got a picture of me," Mitsi said. "She already sent me the photo she took that last day."

"I have no idea." Mom shook her head. "Maybe from the school?"

Mitsi circled her neck with the chain, and secured the clasp. It felt as cool and light as she'd imagined. "How does it look?"

"Lovely," said Mom.

"Very grown up," added the mail lady.

Mom started to toss the wrappings in the trash.

"Oh, it looks like there's something else in here," she said. "A note."

"From Mrs. Bowker." Mitsi grinned. "Or Dash." She flipped it open. But she'd guessed wrong. This note was written in a familiar loopy hand.

Mitsi was so surprised that she couldn't help reading it right there.

Dear Mitsi,

First, I want to say I'm sorry. I wish I had never gone along with Patty. And not just because she and Judy are now thick as thieves. The way she treated you was awful. Well, I treated you pretty bad, too. You might not believe me, but I never put any notes in your desk. That was Patty. But I did take some out. As many as I could.

I wanted to write you when you left, but was pretty sure you'd throw away any letter I sent. (Not that I would've blamed you.) So when I saw Mrs. Bowker out walking Dash one day, I got an idea. And she thought it was a good one. (She's a very nice lady, but I didn't tell her the whole story. At least not at first.) She even let me use her type-writer so you wouldn't recognize my handwriting.

We picked out the locket together. I thought this one would be the one you'd want. And I cut your picture out of one of our old peek-a-boo cards to put inside.

Anyway, I wouldn't blame you for not wanting to be my friend anymore. But, no matter what, I will always be yours.

Love,

Mags

Mitsi could not believe it. Mags took notes out of her desk! She didn't put them in. And she was writing for Dash. Not Mrs. Bowker.

Wait until Debbie heard the good news! Mitsi watched for her in the dining room, but she never came down for supper. And there was no reply when Mitsi pushed a note through their knothole at bedtime.

She ran over to the Miyakes' apartment before breakfast the next morning.

Debbie opened the door, still in her nightgown. "It's awfully early," she said. "Mom's not feeling very good."

"I'm sorry." Mitsi touched her new locket. "I just wanted to show you something."

"I don't feel like playing today." Debbie started to close the door.

"Wait!" Mitsi put her hand out. "Are you mad at me?"

Debbie leaned hard against the door as if she couldn't hold herself up. She brushed her eyes and looked at Mitsi. "It didn't work." She choked out the words. "Not even with God on our side." The door closed between them.

. . .

Mitsi was going to have to babysit Davy by herself. "He's a lot for one person to handle," she hinted to Ted.

"I'm busy." He tucked his shirttail into his new corduroys.

"You look pretty spiffy," Mitsi said. "How come?"

Ted ran a comb through his hair. "None of your beeswax."

"Does it have anything to do with Karen Suda?" she teased.

"That's for me to know and you to find out." Ted slid his comb into his back pocket. "Anyway, you know how to entertain Davy," he said.

"How? I can't do any tricks."

Ted reached under her cot and pulled out Mitsi's sketch pad and pencils. "You can with these." He tossed them onto the blanket.

Mitsi didn't think it would do any good, but she took her pad and pencils. And Davy loved it. "Draw a kitty," he ordered. "A cow. A bear." He actually sat still, watching animals emerge from the tips of her pencils. Mitsi drew until her hand was tired. "Here." She gave him a piece of paper and one of her old crayons. "Your turn."

Mrs. Tokuda couldn't believe it when she came home and found Davy happily scribbling away. "You're a magician!" she said as she paid Mitsi. Mitsi remembered that Mrs. Bowker had said the same thing. It did seem to work on Davy. She thought about drawing something for Debbie. Something that might cheer her up. But she didn't think any picture she drew could do that.

Mom and Pop were talking about Mr. Miyake when Mitsi got home. She plopped on her cot, opened her sketch pad, and began to doodle while she listened. Pop had come back from another meeting with the camp superintendent. "He doesn't like this situation any more than we do. He said he'd look into it. And the other cases, too."

Mom had reached over and squeezed Pop's hand. "Thank you." Her eyes glistened. "I can't imagine how I would manage here without you. Those poor women."

Obaachan looked up from her knitting. "What's that?" she asked Mitsi.

"Oh, I'm just goofing around."

"Show me." Obaachan put down her needles to look at the drawing. "Ah, Mr. Hirai's garden. That's nice."

After making such a hit with Davy, Mitsi got the idea to draw a picture for Mr. Hirai, as a thank-you for the getas. "I think the tumbleweed looks like a Brillo pad," Mitsi said. "Not like tumbleweed."

"My grandfather was a painter." Obaachan picked up her needles again. "Very famous in Japan. He said good art comes from seeing with heart."

Mitsi bent over her drawing again. She wasn't quite sure what her grandmother meant by "seeing with heart." She closed her eyes, thinking about watching Mr. Hirai's garden take shape. And about how she and Debbie had helped him. And that got her thinking about Debbie again. And Mr. Miyake. And how much Debbie missed him. Mitsi understood that, missing Dash the way she did. But missing a dog was nothing like missing a father.

Her eyes popped open.

She'd been feeling bad because she wasn't able to do anything for Debbie. But there was something she could do.

• • •

Mrs. Miyake answered the door this time.

Mitsi saw Debbie lying facedown on her cot. "May I come in?"

"Please, yes." Mrs. Miyake stepped aside.

Mitsi moved toward Debbie's cot. "I'm really sorry about your dad," she said.

"Me, too." Debbie sniffled. "I don't feel like company right now." She shifted under the covers.

"You said you had a photo of him, right?" Mitsi moved closer, setting a small blue box on the bedspread. "Maybe this would help you keep him close.

Until you're all together again." She headed back to the door.

"I'll see you later." Mitsi let herself out.

. . .

That night, Mitsi crawled under the covers. Even though she hadn't had it very long, her neck felt bare without the locket. She glanced over at the photo of her and Dash, sitting in its Popsicle-stick frame on her nightstand. With that as a model, she'd started a sketch of Dash that was already even better than the one she'd torn up. Mom said it looked so real, she could almost smell his doggy breath.

She thought about drawing something for Mrs. Bowker and Mags. And Miss Wyatt, too. She rolled over on her side, yawning, ready for sleep.

Something scrabbled around under her cot. Mitsi rolled to the edge and looked underneath. A note slipped through the knothole. Mitsi opened it up and read two wonderful words.

Thank you.

CHAPTER SEVENTEEN

My Brother's Keeper

They went through three teachers in the first three weeks of sixth grade. The first one went into hysterics over the rattler under the steps, even though one of the boys clomped it with his baseball bat before anyone got hurt. The second teacher didn't make it until first recess. When she found out there wasn't even a blackboard in the room, she walked out.

"My mother always said make do or go without," the third teacher announced from behind an enormous stack of books she'd lugged into the classroom. She wrote her name, Miss Pellegrino, in perfect Palmer penmanship on a math worksheet and thumbtacked it to the wall behind her scrap-lumber desk. "*We* will make do." She handed Mitsi a roll of butcher paper. "Get a friend to help hang this up for our blackboard.

"Apply copious amounts of elbow grease," she ordered the boys as she distributed sheets of sandpaper to knock the splinters out of the hewn benches that were both chairs and desk you don't have a job yet, find one," she comman the rest of the class. "Together we will turn t humble space into a hallowed palace of learning.'

Recess was a "field trip" to gather tumbleweed greasewood, and stones for a "natural sciences corner." Everyone came back to the classroom dusty and triumphant with their finds, even Miss Pellegrino. Debbie showed off the scorpion she'd captured in a tin cup. "Marvelous!" Their teacher promptly assigned reports on desert wildlife. With that mole on her cheek and hair so thin you could see her scalp, Miss Pellegrino was a bit odd-looking, but Mitsi felt pretty sure she would stick it out. At least, she hoped she would.

After lunch, Miss Pellegrino discovered a box of donated books under a pile of scrap lumber, and nearly swooned. "First thing tomorrow, we will set up a class library. Who can tell me about the Dewey Decimal system?" There were twenty-seven kids in the sixth grade and twenty-seven kids hung around at the end of the school day, afraid they might miss something.

At four o'clock, Miss Pellegrino shooed them all home. "I'll be here tomorrow," she said. "Will you?" Mitsi certainly would. One of the books on Miss Pellegrino's desk was *The Boys and Girls Beginning Book of Drawing*; Mitsi couldn't wait to get a good look at that. So far, school was the best thing about Minidoka.

Debbie loaned Mitsi the "O" encyclopedia so she could read about the animal she'd chosen for her report, the burrowing owl. "I'm doing my report on Scorpy," Debbie said. She'd scavenged a mayonnaise jar from the dining hall for the scorpion's home. "I might have to catch him a mouse." She shivered.

Mitsi read over her shoulder. "It says they also eat insects. Maybe he'll be happy with bugs."

Debbie made a face. "I hope so."

Back in her own apartment, Mitsi stretched out on her cot with a pillow propped behind her back, and Chubby Bear at her side, reading about burrowing owls. It was another one of those rare nights when baby Louise next door was quiet and the rest of her family was busy. Mom and Pop were at another meeting about the coal situation and she was pretty sure Obaachan was knitting with the dried-plum ladies. And Ted was AWOL.

Mitsi turned the page. There was a picture of a burrowing owl in flight. It was as real as a photo, but someone had drawn it. She'd like to be able to draw like that, too, someday. She thought about what Eddie Sato had told her before he left Camp Harmony. "I'm not any more talented than the next guy. It's like anything else. Practice makes perfect." Mitsi studied the picture, then reached for her pad and began to draw. The page was covered with erasures as she tried to get the feathers right.

She nearly jumped off her cot when the door slammed open.

Ted sauntered into the room, tugging his baseball cap over his left eye.

"You about gave me a heart attack." Mitsi picked up the pencil she'd dropped.

"I thought you'd be over at Debbie's."

"We have homework."

Ted shot her a glance. "Homework? For that Mickey Mouse school?"

"It's not — hey." The sketch pad fell to her lap. "What happened to you?"

Ted turned away from her, trying to hide his black eye. "I misjudged a fly."

"You were playing baseball? In the dark?" Mitsi got up from the cot. "Let me see."

"Drop it, Mits." Ted brushed her away. "I'll put a cold cloth on it. It'll be fine." He stomped back out of the apartment.

Mitsi would not call a black eye fine. She knew one thing for sure: When she was a mom, she wasn't going to believe one word her kids told her. She tugged on her Keds and stomped out after her brother.

He'd disappeared into the latrines. She waited. Ted was right. The men's really did stink. She pinched her nose, breathing through her mouth.

Ted stopped when he came out and saw her. "What is your problem?"

"My problem?" Mitsi blinked back tears. "You."

Ted pushed past her. "I can take care of myself."

"I am my brother's keeper." She sniffled, repeating a verse they'd learned in Sunday school. She thought he'd storm off. But he didn't.

"I don't need keeping."

Mitsi ran the back of her hand under her nose. "You know what I wish?"

"What?" Ted took off his baseball cap and turned it around in his hands.

"I wish I was a good magician. Like you. So I could turn you back into my real brother." She held her breath.

Ted laughed. "You goof. I am your real brother." He set his cap on top of her head. "Things are going to be fine. Trust me."

She straightened the cap. "I do."

"And listen. That dumb story you read that time?"

"*Thimble Summer*?"

"I bet the girl went back and told the librarian what she'd done. Paid her for the candy she took. Am I right?"

Mitsi rubbed away the moisture on her cheeks. "Yeah. That's right, Magic. That's right."

He took his cap back. "I'm Ted. Plain old Ted."

• • •

The dining hall buzzed with the news. Lefty sat by himself with his oatmeal, wearing a shiner that mirrored Ted's. By the time Mitsi finished her corn flakes, she'd heard the whole story. Lefty and a couple other guys confessed to the robbery. She couldn't help but wonder if those black eyes meant that Ted had something to do with Lefty's confession. The boys gave back the money and were sentenced to two months of latrine detail. And though Ted was sitting at a different table, making puppy-dog eyes at Karen Suda across the room, Mitsi had her brother back. He was even planning to put on a magic show for the little kids for Halloween.

After Miss Pellegrino had tacked Mitsi's burrowing owl drawing to the wall, right behind her desk, other kids in the class asked Mitsi to draw pictures for *their* desert animal reports. Mitsi began to carry her sketch pad and pencils with her everywhere, drawing different camp scenes.

Sometimes, she gave the drawings away. Like the one of the dining hall for the Cauliflower Cook. But most of them she kept for her scrapbook. These weren't the kind of memories she'd expected to be saving, but like Eddie Sato had said, it was important to remember. To remember everything.

Mitsi put the finishing touches on a drawing of their apartment, as it had looked when they'd first arrived, covered in dust. Right before she mailed it off to Mags, she added a caption at the bottom of the page: *In the camp, we got plenty of Vitamin D. D for Dust.* She thought Eddie would approve. She smiled, then folded up the drawing and put it in an envelope.

She tied on her Keds and stepped outside. She knocked on Debbie's door. Obaachan was right. There were some things that could not be helped. Like getting sent to the camps. Mitsi had no choice about that. But she did have a choice about what she made of it. Like Mr. Hirai creating a beautiful garden out of ugly old tumbleweed.

The door swung open. Her good friend stood there, silver locket sparkling on her neck. "Let me guess. You're heading to the post office?"

Mitsi smiled. "Want to come along?"

Debbie closed the door behind her. "Do you even need to ask?"

CHAPTER EIGHTEEN
Special Deliveries

The new art teacher, Mrs. Light, asked Mitsi's class to help the first graders make pinecone turkeys for the holiday. Mitsi and Debbie were gluing tail feathers when the principal knocked at their classroom door.

"Debbie?" he said. "Will you come with me?"

Debbie wiped her sticky hands on a rag, and followed the principal out of the room. At the door, she glanced back at Mitsi. Mitsi could read her mind. Had the principal found out about the prank they'd pulled in the dining hall? That lizard had slid right off the Jell-O tray; the cook even laughed. Were they going to get in trouble anyway?

Seconds later, Debbie ran back in, locket bouncing at her neck. She wore a huge smile. "He's here!" was all she said. Then she grabbed her coat and was gone.

At supper, Debbie and her mother walked into the dining hall, on either side of a thin man in glasses. "This is my dad." Debbie held his arm so tightly that he could hardly shake hands with Pop.

"So — you are Mitsi." Debbie's father bowed. "Thank you for being such a good friend to Debbie."

"It's been lovely to meet you." Mom tugged Mitsi away. "But we're sure you'd like some time to catch up." Obaachan made her way over to join the dried-plum ladies. Ted was still delivering the *Irrigator*, but when he came in, Mitsi was pretty sure he'd sit with that new group of junior high guys. A nicer group, but still boys. Loud and rowdy.

Mitsi sat between Mom and Pop, a different kind of Mitsi sandwich. Because of the camps, life was never going to be the same. But that didn't mean that life couldn't be okay.

She was cutting her gristly Salisbury steak when Ted hurried over. Before he could speak, she told him the news about Debbie's father.

"It's better than Christmas," she said.

"You can say that again." Ted pulled a copy of the *Irrigator* from his back pocket and flipped it onto the table in front of her. Mitsi couldn't believe what she read.

She ran back to their apartment without even touching her dessert. She had a letter to write!

Dear Dash,

This is a double good news day. First: Debbie's dad is here. Now they really are a true family again.

You'll never guess, but the second good news has to do with you!

General DeWitt says that we can have pets! Of course, we have to ask for permission from the camp superintendent, but he's a nice man. I know he won't say no.

Love, Mitsi

• • •

Mitsi had hurried off without her mittens, so she blew into her cupped hands to warm up. Every time she saw a cloud of exhaust steam from the road, she was sure this was it. But each time, it was the wrong car.

Maybe something had happened. A flat tire. A broken radiator. Maybe even an accident. She shivered, then started pacing back and forth across the main road to warm up. She crossed eight, nine, ten times. She leaned over the gate as far as she could.

Maybe they wouldn't come today after all. She wrapped her arms around herself, huddling against the December cold.

"Ruff, ruff."

Mitsi's head flew up. She'd recognize that bark anywhere. A fluffy almond-colored head leaned out of the passenger window of the car stopped at the sentry post.

The sentry waved the car through. Mitsi ran toward it. "Dash!" She splashed across the slushy, muddy path. "Dash!"

The car stopped and the door opened. A streak of fur bolted out and right into her arms. Mitsi lost her balance and almost fell on her backside. Laughing, she wrapped her arms around her dog. He nearly wiggled right out of her arms, whimpering and trying to cover her face in dog kisses. He had doggy breath. Delicious doggy breath.

"He missed you." Mrs. Bowker stood next to the car, her black galoshes already brick red with mud.

Mitsi squeezed Dash even tighter. "I missed him, too." She knew she should say "Thank you" to Mrs. Bowker. But her throat closed up and no more words would come out. She buried her face in Dash's fur. He still smelled like a well-worn penny.

"We drove as fast as we could once we heard from you." Mrs. Bowker wiped her eyes with a hanky.

The driver of the car stepped forward. "That's quite a dog you've got there," he said. "He really won Mother over. I wasn't sure she would be able to give him back!"

Mitsi's heart stopped. "Oh —" She'd never thought Mrs. Bowker might end up loving Dash as much as she did.

"Oh, Alan, don't tease." Mrs. Bowker pretended to give the man a swat, as if he were a little kid. "Mitsi, this is my son."

Mitsi nodded, still unable to breathe. Her ears began to ring, like they had before she'd gotten used to the altitude.

Mrs. Bowker placed her hands on Mitsi's coat sleeves, and looked her straight in the eyes. "Even though my house will be too quiet without him, I am delighted you and Dash are back together."

Mitsi finally took a breath. "Was he a good boy?"

Mrs. Bowker laughed. "Well, I have a few holes in my garden that I didn't plan on, but other than that, he was the perfect houseguest."

Mitsi finally remembered her manners. "Mom has some cookies. And tea. Come with me."

"That would be lovely." Mrs. Bowker reached back into the car and retrieved a brown paper bag. "Better not forget Dash's suitcase!" She rummaged in the bag and brought out his leash. "Would you like this so you don't have to carry him?"

Later, Mitsi would take him for a walk around the camp. Introduce him to Debbie and Mr. Hirai. Show Davy his tricks.

But for right now, Mitsi didn't need the leash. She wasn't about to put him down.

Mitsi started for her family's block. Mrs. Bowker and Alan followed.

"Good boy, Dash." Mitsi scratched behind his ears, just the way he liked. "Good dog."

AUTHOR'S NOTE

After the Japanese Navy attacked Pearl Harbor on December 7, 1941, Americans were worried and afraid. It was a hard time for everyone, but hardest of all for the Japanese immigrants and Japanese Americans, *Nikkei*, living on the West Coast of the United States. Some newspapers and elected officials insisted that the Nikkei would help Japan, and managed to convince others that they were a danger to our country. In February 1942, President Franklin D. Roosevelt signed Executive Order 9066 authorizing the exclusion of "any or all persons" from designated military areas. But "any or all" really meant people of German, Italian, or Japanese descent. Within a month, the focus had shifted away from the Germans and Italians to people of Japanese descent, and FDR signed Executive Order 9012, creating ten War Relocation camps, to be built in different parts of the country. Nearly 120,000 Nikkei, most of them American citizens, were sent away to those camps.

One of them was a lady named Mitsue "Mitsi" Shiraishi, who loved her dog, Chubby, very much. Mitsi wrote to General John L. DeWitt, the man in charge of the evacuation, asking if she could bring Chubby along to the camp. Though that letter has been lost, we know General DeWitt's office answered with a no. A neighbor, Mrs. Charles Bovee, took care of Chubby for Mitsi. Mrs. Bovee kept a diary of his first week in the Bovee household.

She made it seem as if Chubby himself had written the diary. It was her way of reassuring Mitsi that her beloved pet was happy and cared for in his new, temporary home. One of the entries said, *Tonight . . . we had such a good time. While the others planted dahlias, I ran all around the lawn and scampered back and forth until I was ready to go in the house and lie on the floor in front of the fireplace. I have been rather upset the last hour for every time I go to the door there is a little dog just like me in the glass in the door. When I bark, he barks too and doesn't seem to be a bit ashamed to think he is such a copycat.*

About a year after Mitsi went to camp (she was sent to Tule Lake, not Minidoka, as was the Mitsi of this story), the rules were relaxed. People were allowed to have pets, and Mitsi was reunited with her furry friend.

Like Mitsi, and maybe like many of you, I also have a dog. Winston also barks at the strange dog in the glass, completely unaware that he's barking at his own reflection. He's crazy about playing ball and jumps straight up in the air when I bring one out. His favorite game is to chase the ball and bring it back to me. Well, most of the time, he brings it back. I can barely stand to be apart from Winston for one day. I can't imagine how hard it was for Mitsi to be separated from Chubby when she had no idea how long the separation would last. After I heard their story, I began to think about all of the Nikkei — especially the children — who were forced to leave their pets behind when they were sent to the war relocation camps.

Every story needs a heart hook, and that was mine.

ACKNOWLEDGMENTS

Thank you to Dave Neiwert for his book *Strawberry Days*, which is where I first read about Mitsi and Chubby. I am grateful to Judy Kusakabe, Mitsi Shiraishi's step-daughter, for lending me her family's memorabilia (including Chubby's diary), and am honored that they'd share such special treasures with me; to Debbie and Louise Kashino for so many helpful introductions and for allowing me to borrow their surname; and to Louis Fiset, author of *Camp Harmony: Japanese American Internment and the Puyallup Assembly Center*, who shared his precious map of Camp Harmony with a complete stranger, and simply because I asked.

If you want to know more about life at Camp Harmony or at Minidoka, visit Densho.org. That is where I was introduced to Eddie Sato, whose sketches realistically yet humorously captured camp life. Eddie did indeed incorporate an ant into his signature.

None of my books would exist without Mary Nethery, trusted first reader; Neil Larson, cheerleader extraordinaire; and Jill Grinberg, the world's best agent.

But this book owes its largest debt to Lisa Sandell, who immediately said yes when she heard about Mitsi and who, once again, gently drew out of me a much stronger story than I ever thought possible.

ABOUT THE AUTHOR

Kirby Larson is the acclaimed author of the 2007 Newbery Honor book *Hattie Big Sky*; its sequel, *Hattie Ever After*; *The Friendship Doll*; Dear America: *The Fences Between Us*; *Duke*; *Liberty*; and *Audacity Jones to the Rescue*. She has also cowritten two award-winning picture books about dogs, including *Two Bobbies: A True Story of Hurricane Katrina, Friendship, and Survival* and *Nubs: The True Story of a Mutt, a Marine & a Miracle*. She lives in Washington State with her husband and Winston the Wonder Dog.

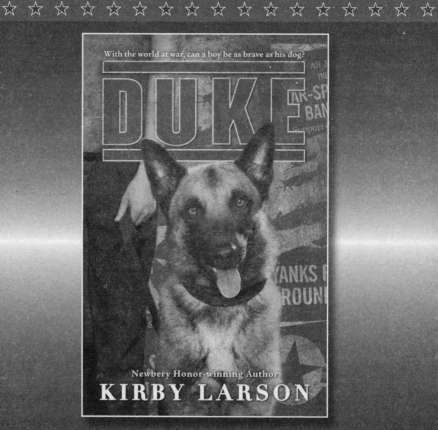